ART OF RETRIBUTION

Thrillers by Millicent Hodge

Abuse of Power
Absence of Justice

Art of Retribution
Act of Vengeance

Copyright © 2003 by Capitol Ventures Assoc., LLC
Library of Congress Number: 2003093419
ISBN: Hardcover   1-4134-1159-2
Softcover   1-4134-1158-4

This book was printed in the United States of America.
Jacket and Interior Images by Index Stock Imagery
Visit the author's website at: www.MillicentHodge.com

To order additional copies of this book, visit:
www.Amazon.com

19174

To my nieces and nephews,
may you have wonderful lives.

**If you sit by the river long enough,
the bodies of your enemies will float by.**

—Author Unknown

THE VERDICT

WASHINGTON, D.C.

October

Wednesday morning. "The verdict is in."
The inmate did not move. He sat on a lower bunk bed, staring at a cinder block wall. His index finger traced the deep, pinkish-red scars on his face. Four months earlier, he had placed the cool barrel of a pistol to his head and pulled the trigger.

"Hell-o?" The prison guard inched closer.

Silence.

"Hey, Rog, did you hear me?" The guard tipped into the ten-by-twelve cell. The jingle of his keys echoed in the maximum security unit. "Hey, Roger Dodger?" The guard rested his scrawny hip against the dense metal door and fished for a cigarette in his baggy gray uniform. He found lint and frowned. After a minute, he slithered closer. He stopped, took a deep breath, and then leaned down cautiously, peering at the man's scars. "Damn man," he scrunched up his pale face, "you ought to think about getting that fixed." He leaned closer, scratching his unshaven bristles.

Roger Alexander turned suddenly, giving the guard the full heat of his stare.

"Ahhh!" yelped the guard, jumping back to the door, a nervous smile on his face. "Holy shit, it's moving." He turned, shouting down the corridor. "If anybody sees my head roll out there, call 911. I'm down here with Lucifer." He giggled, but kept his feet near the door.

Alexander turned away.

"All us guards are taking bets on you," he grinned. "Me? I put my money on the electric chair." He lowered his butt as if sitting in a chair and wiggled it. "Ewww," he said, leaping out of the imaginary chair. "That's a little hot." He howled with laughter.

Alexander did not blink.

"If there is any justice at all, they'd fry you up by turkey day." The guard flapped his arms. "Gobble, gobble, gobble."

Alexander turned on a small silver radio. Classical music flowed into the cell.

The guard's sneer faded and he puffed out his small chest. "Okay, dammit. Get up." Metal clinked as he looked down and snatched a pair of handcuffs from his belt. "It's time to go."

The guard never saw the big man rise like a shot and snatch him up by the throat. "Oh—" His feet dangled in the air as he gasped for air. "We don't . . . have . . . to leave . . . right this minute. Maybe—" His back slammed into a wall. The veins in his neck bulged. "If I've offended you in some—" He could barely breathe as Alexander squeezed. The guard's face turned reddish-blue as he clutched the handcuffs at his side.

"I'll take those."

Roger Alexander watched the guard struggle to turn his head toward the voice coming from the doorway. It was deep and male. Alexander shifted, lining his right eye up with the door. A bullet had ripped through his head, severing an optic nerve in the other eye. Within seconds, a clean-shaven head appeared in Alexander's sole line of vision. The eye showed a lean man with medium brown skin, brown eyes and a moustache trimmed in a neat square around his mouth. Alexander dropped the guard, coughing and gasping.

"Like the man said, it's time to go."

Sitting down on the bed, Alexander finally spoke. "Charles."

"Alexander."

Alexander watched the other man regard him. He knew his black hair was thinner, as was his bulky, six-two frame, currently in an orange jumpsuit stamped Lynnwood Correctional Facility. His skin was pallid; his wide face deeply scarred. His left eye was sutured shut, but one small dark eye revealed ego and anger. He knew this from staring into a mirror during his solitary confinement.

"Deputy Director Thomas," said Alexander. "I hear congratulations will soon be in order. Who would have ever thought it?"

"The President would and did," said Thomas.

"I guess the gold earring didn't befit your new status," said Alexander, without moving. On the day he shot himself, Thomas had leaned against a courtroom wall wearing a gold stud earring. A quiet and intense man, he had exploded the hearing with new evidence. For his troubles, Charles Thomas would soon be promoted to FBI Director.

"President Wright frowned on it."

"How is my former boss?" asked Alexander.

"He sends his regards."

"Did he send you here personally to pick me up?"

"As a matter of fact, he did," said Thomas, stepping into the small cell. "And I was happy to do it."

Alexander held his gaze. "Well, I'm not going."

"The hell you aren't." Thomas held his hand out, palm up. "Give me those cuffs," he said to the skinny guard, who stopped wheezing long enough to glance from one man to the other. The steel clinked as the handcuffs dropped into his palm. "As soon as I slap this prison jewelry on you, we're out of here."

"I said—"

Deputy Director Thomas nodded and six FBI agents appeared. Like him, they wore black uniforms with bullet-proof vests. Alexander's dark eye shifted. Cornered, he focused on a vest. "Do I get one of those?"

"Of course," said Thomas. "We don't want another Jack Ruby, do we?"

Alexander blinked.

Fifteen minutes later and escorted by heavily armed FBI agents, Alexander shuffled out the prison door, straining against the thick leg irons. He glanced down at the manacles wrapped tightly around his hands and waist. The metal creased his new suit. The bullet-proof vest underneath only made the chains tighter. He seethed with cold rage. He had waged and won a small battle to wear the navy business suit instead of the orange jumpsuit. Now that it was ruined, he wanted to hurt somebody. He had no control over his own life. His telephone calls were recorded. His meals regulated. His urine samples tested. He was controlled by imbeciles. Under any other circumstances, he would have broken that little pissant's neck earlier, for taunting him like a child.

Alexander glanced forward at the solid back of Thomas. This was his fault. And for that, Alexander hated him. He loathed everyone who had turned on him. Ambling forward, Alexander stepped out of the shadows into the fall sunshine. He smelled burning leaves. His fury waned as he turned his scarred face into the cool breeze. He had not been outside the seven-facility complex in months. Within seconds, he was hoisted into a waiting black van. Agents piled in behind him and slammed the doors shut.

Avoiding the watchful eyes of the Deputy Director, Alexander rocked forward as the van passed a barbed wire fence and started down the narrow road leading away from the decaying red-brick prison. He burned to see outside, but the back of the van was barren steel and windowless. Instead, Alexander's gaze moved across the faces of the agents surrounding him. They stared back, hands on weapons. He knew there was no chance of escape, so he fixed his dark eye on a television set, a small portable nestled in the far corner.

Thomas motioned to an agent who kneeled and flicked through the channels. Every broadcast was about Alexander, but only one reporter stood on the courthouse steps. Alexander's tongue slid along his lower lip as he recognized her sapphire blue eyes. Her hair lifted due to the crisp breeze. He recalled two occasions when her hair, champagne blonde and long, had draped over his shoulder as she whispered suggestive comments into his ear. Both times, he had stood and abruptly left the room. He had been powerful, but preferred his women submissive. Now, however, he was unemployed, incarcerated and disfigured. He shrugged his shoulders and watched her electric blue skirt flutter against her firm thighs.

"I'm reporting live from the United States District Courthouse," said the reporter. "According to my sources, the jury has finally reached a verdict. Only moments ago, they filed into courtroom number fifteen. Inside the federal building behind me—" she turned, appeared to catch her breath and pointed to a six-story, white limestone building with E. Barrett Prettyman Courthouse inscribed across the top, "the jury has made a decision in this, the death penalty phase of the murder trial. As you know, they deliberated for three days, putting in more than fourteen hours per day. The nation has been enthralled. And we are now breathlessly awaiting the jury's life-or-death decision."

As Alexander watched, the reporter glanced behind her as throngs of other reporters and camera crews arrived and crowded onto the plaza around her. Nearby, uniformed police set up blue barricades to restrain the herd. Overhead, two American flags fluttered against the crisp blue sky. Alexander's gaze returned to the reporter.

Appearing to press an earpiece in her ear, she paused and then said, "The former Deputy Attorney General of the United States is on his way to the courthouse right now." She paused again. "I'm being told the FBI van has just left Lynnwood Prison in Fairfax, Virginia, and is heading this way, toward the District of Columbia. Perhaps, we can get a live helicopter shot of that."

Rocking forward in the van, Alexander heard chopping sounds overhead. He lifted his eye to the metal ceiling of the van. Circling lower, the helicopter's blades sliced into the wind. He looked down at the television set. There was an overhead shot of the black van crawling up Interstate 95. It was surrounded by FBI vehicles and white police cars, with Virginia and Washington emblems, and whirling red and blue lights. As sirens wailed from both the television set and from outside, he felt reality and fantasy mix.

Alexander blinked as the newscast cut back to the reporter, "As widely reported," she said, "Roger Alexander was recently convicted of murder. During a six-week trial, the U. S. Attorney presented a lean and compelling case. The twelve-member federal jury was obviously persuaded by the prosecutor during the guilt phase of this trial. After the prosecutor won her guilty verdict—a unanimous verdict—she implored the jury to sentence Alexander to death. If sentenced to die, he will be one of only twenty-seven federal prisoners on death row. Roger Alexander could become the fourth federal prisoner to be executed since 1963."

"All rise." The bailiff rose, eyes scanning the packed courtroom. His hand gripped the gun holstered at the side of his brown uniform. While he waited for hushed whispers to cease, the wall clock, above his head, ticked to nine thirty in the morning. Nervous, his eyes met those of Alexander and then swept over the federal courtroom. All hell had broken loose the last time these people were gathered here. "Court is now in session," he said. "The Honorable Ann Lombard presiding."

Wielding a stylish brown cane, Judge Lombard swept into the courtroom and up the stairs to the elevated brown bench. Her soft, silver-gray hair was swept up into a neat bun. "This is case number 2246," she said, sitting down. Her long black robe ruffled. "The United States versus Roger Alexander."

For the moment, she ignored both the jurors and the defendant. She peered over her reading glasses. The press was packed into rows of polished brown benches; the rest stood, lining the white walls. Their eyes and pens moved feverishly, absorbing everything. "Let me start by stating that cameras are still banned from my courtroom." Her speech was a deliberate Cajun cadence, cultivated in a poor farming community in Louisiana. "Furthermore, there will be no outbursts at the reading of the verdict. Anyone found violating this rule will be held in contempt of court and carted off to jail." Lombard glanced at the bailiff. When she looked back at the spectators, she was met by meek stares and silence. Her dim blue eyes shifted and then bore into the small dark eye of the former Deputy Attorney General. "Will the defendant please rise?" demanded the judge.

Alexander pushed back his chair. As he stood, he glanced over his thick shoulder. Everyone responsible for his destruction was seated in the sixth-floor courtroom. He met their stares. He was slowly drawn into a contest of wills by one intense gaze. The eyes were still, unyielding. He had considered whether she would be here. On his last day of freedom, she had warned him, "It's not over until I win." He felt his attorney's firm hand on his shoulder. Alexander turned to face the judge. His eye moved from the raised bench, which stood between two American flags, up the twenty-foot-high wall behind the judge. The emerald granite backdrop bore the gold United States seal encircling the American bald eagle. His eye moved back to the judge. She would soon ascend to the Supreme Court. They had all risen from his fall.

"Mr. Alexander," said the judge, leaning forward, "you were convicted of a single count of murder in the first degree. You did willingly, with malicious aforethought, take the life of another human being. If that were not horrific enough, you brought that evil through the doors of this very courtroom." Her eyes scanned her room. Seated before her, the court reporter's head bobbed, dark curly hair covering her olive face, as her fingers flew over the stenograph keyboard. Reporters seated in the hushed courtroom scribbled wildly. She glanced at the pale green carpet where spots of reddish-brown blood had been removed, and then back at the defendant. "Before a room filled with witnesses, you shot Peter Savant."

Alexander's heart raced as he envisioned the short barrel, the pearl handle and the powerful blast. He glanced at the prosecution table and met the intense gray eyes of the federal prosecutor. His former employee tucked a wisp of short blonde hair behind her ear and averted her eyes.

Alexander looked forward as the judge said, "Under Chapter 49, Section 1111 of the Federal Criminal Code, whoever is guilty of murder in the first degree shall be punished by life imprisonment—" she paused, "or by death." His gaze followed hers to the jury box. "Members of the jury, have you reached a verdict in the death penalty phase of this trial?"

Alexander scanned the diverse faces of the jury. Seated in two rows of brown leather chairs, they avoided his stare. Alexander had allegedly dumped the body of a grand juror into the Potomac River, but no one could prove it. The twelve jurors focused on the judge.

"Yes, we have, Your Honor." Standing, the jury foreman nervously smoothed her yellow skirt.

"Please hand your verdict to the bailiff."

The bailiff crossed the room, took the written verdict and handed it to the judge. The judge opened the paper, read it without expression, glanced at the jury foreman, who was sitting down, and then handed it back to the bailiff. "The verdict is in proper order," said the judge. She watched the bailiff cross the room and hand the paper back to the foreman. "Again," said the judge, scanning the room, "I caution all present to avoid any reaction to the findings of this verdict. Anyone violating the rules of my court will be removed." She waited for the bailiff to return to his post and place his hand on his weapon. Then she said, "Jury foreman, please read the verdict."

As the foreman slowly rose to her feet, her dark eyes darted around the courtroom. "By unanimous vote, we sentence the defendant, Roger Martin Alexander . . . to death."

Alexander sank to his chair, ignoring the uproar. Blood pulsed in his ears as cheering erupted. Sights and sounds dissolved into echoes and shadows. Why was he the only one paying the price?

Judge Lombard banged her brown gavel as reporters scrambled out of the double doors. "I want order in this courtroom." The din subsided. She glared at her courtroom. Silence. She turned to the jury box. "So say you one, so say you all?"

"Yes, Your Honor," replied the jurors in unison.

Still staring ahead, Alexander felt his attorney jump to his feet. The lawyer requested a polling of the jurors.

"Let's have a polling of the jurors," said Judge Lombard.

One by one, each juror rose and said, "Death."

THE WINNER TAKES ALL

CHAPTER 2

Wednesday midmorning. Sidney Cox gazed at the team of lawyers seated across the long table. "Is your client taking the deal or not?" she demanded. She was flanked by as many investigators and attorneys from the FBI-DEA Joint Task Force. The conference room on the sixth floor of the courthouse crackled with tension.

"Roger Alexander was sentenced to death less than thirty minutes ago and you're already focused on the next trial?" said Nathaniel Drake.

"It's the President's first priority."

"Then we're here because the midterm elections are next week?"

"It was your client's decision to sign a joint defense agreement with Alexander," said Sidney.

Her eyes shifted from the lawyer to his client. He was attempting to look casual, without a suit jacket, in a rolled-up, steam-pressed, white-sleeved shirt, red suspenders and Gucci loafers. However, his thin face was paler than usual and his fingers had not stopped running through his fine, ash blond hair. Until recently, he had not spent much time in rooms like this one. It was large, rectangular, and bare. The white walls were more yellow than white. The conference table was brown and nicked. The windows facing Constitution Avenue were grimy with dusty venetian blinds. The scratched coat rack was leaning to one side, weighed down by trench coats and jackets. The floor was white linoleum and there was a single brown door leading to an outer office. Studying Bruce, she noted the fear and frustration in his bluish-gray eyes. Before he had betrayed her, she had considered him a friend. For that matter, she had worked with several of the lawyers seated across from her. Until further notice, they were now all suspect in her mind.

"That's not a crime," said Drake, the lead lawyer for the other side.

Sidney's eyes shifted back to him. "That remains to be seen."

"You've got nothing."

"Are your certain?" asked Sidney.

"What you do have is a conflict, Ms. Cox," said Drake, leaning forward. Tall, trim and courtly with silver hair, his eyes were steady. "You were fired from Drake, Spaulding & Lloyd. And you were formally the target of this very investigation."

"What you have, Mr. Drake, is the head of this investigation." She leaned forward. "Appointed by the President of the United States. If you think I have a conflict, I suggest you take it up with him."

From the corner of her eye, Sidney noticed her team lean forward, all eyes focused across the table. She then watched Drake visually canvass the room. He met the firm stares of the heads of the Drug Enforcement Agency, the FBI, the District Police Department, and the sharpest attorneys and investigators from the U.S. Justice Department. He did not blink, but his eyes did return to her face.

"If you had any evidence on my client," he said, "you would have prosecuted him along with Roger Alexander."

"Sometimes the best legal strategy is the simplest strategy." She set her elbows on the table and folded her hands. "We had Roger Alexander cold on the Savant murder. He shot the man in the chest in open court in front of a room full of witnesses. Open, shut, pull the lever," she said. "It was my decision to pursue a two-trial strategy. It was the decision of the U.S. Attorney for the District of Columbia to request the death penalty." Without noticing it, she sighed at the thought of the woman who had won the death conviction. She would be impossible to live with now that she had secured this verdict. "However, now that we have a death sentence against Alexander, it's time to move on to the real heart of the matter." She locked eyes with his client. So far, he had taken his right to remain silent very seriously, but she suspected that her former boss would break soon.

"The drug trial?" asked Drake.

"And the murder of the Attorney General," said Sidney Cox. Her eyes never wavered.

"Sidney," pleaded Bruce Lewis, "you know I didn't kill the Attorney General. I wasn't even there. I—"

Drake held up his hand, cutting off his client. "What he knows and where he was is of no consequence," said Drake. He glanced at his team of associates. They each carried large black elephant bags filled with legal documents. What documents they carried depended solely on which of Drake's three clients they were assigned. "You've got no evidence. You've got no witnesses," said Drake. "First, any disks that may have been on Roger Alexander when he shot himself were incinerated at the hospital with his bloody clothes. Second, if there was any evidence on his laptop computer, you have yet to produce it. And third, no court in the country is going to let in that alleged taped confession. It's been spliced more than a rap video. You may be winning in the court of public opinion, but that's not where we intend to play this game."

"We've got a witness," said Sidney.

Attorney and client leaned forward. "Who?" asked the lawyer. Sidney was silent.

"You're required to turn over any evidence that you have to us," said Drake. His team of young lawyers, all wearing crisp blue or black suits, nodded in unison.

"Your client hasn't been charged with anything yet." Sidney shifted focus. "Who is the architect of your joint defense strategy?" asked Sidney. "You?"

"Why do you ask?"

"We find it odd that the same criminal defense team represents Roger Alexander, your client here, as well as Christina Savant."

"Is that why you've set up these three interviews today?"

"Why would Christina Savant throw in her fate, and the fate

of her newly inherited conglomerate, with the folks who shot her brother? Strikes me as odd."

"They have similar interests."

"Really?" asked Sidney. "And what would those be?" She watched him regard her in silence. "And will they have similar verdicts?" She glanced from the lawyer to his client. The client blinked twice. "We've got an indictment against you," she said.

"What!" said Bruce.

"When?" asked Drake, clearing his throat.

"Ten minutes ago," said Sidney. "Twenty minutes after Alexander, your other client, was sentenced to death." She reached into a folder. "Here's a copy of the indictment." She slid the true bill across the table.

Drake caught it and opened it. As he read, his eyebrows gathered.

Bruce leaned over the copy. He blinked rapidly as he read the written accusation in his lawyer's hands. "You're charging me with conspiring to import cocaine and heroin into the United States?" Tiny beads of perspiration appeared on his forehead.

"It triggers the federal death penalty," said Sidney.

"You can't be serious," said Bruce.

Sidney glanced at a young woman seated behind her. The assistant's long brownish-black hair swung forward as she handed several documents to Sidney. As Sidney slid a document across the table, she said, "Here's a copy of the Anti-Drug Abuse Act of 1988." She watched Drake catch the document. "Here's a copy of the Federal Death Penalty Act of 1994." She slid that document across the table. "Congress imposed the death penalty for sixty different offenses under thirteen existing and twenty-eight newly-created federal capital statutes. It includes narcotic offenses, drug-related killings and political assassinations." She rested her hands on top of the table. "We're very serious."

Bruce's eyes flew around the room. "There's no death penalty in the District of Columbia."

"Stay focused, Bruce," said Sidney. "This is under the *federal* statute." She watched his chest expand as he tried to breathe.

Perspiration rolled down his forehead as he stared at the document lying before him. When she blinked, the pale blue eyes of the Attorney General flashed in her mind. Sweat had suddenly appeared on his brow as he lay dying. She blinked again and the memory vanished. She watched Bruce's face as he grasped the full implications of his situation. Earlier this morning, she had watched Roger Alexander the same way as his verdict was read. She had successfully turned the tables on them. With the support of her parents, friends and several of the people seated beside her, she had won. She glanced out of the row of windows, watching traffic turn off Third Street onto Constitution Avenue. Bluish-gray sunlight bathed the U.S. Capitol. People flowed in and out of the nearby museums and the Department of Labor. As they rushed to work, she knew that they were unaware that Bruce's life had changed forever in that one instance. However, they would all read about it tomorrow morning in the *Washington Post*. His name would never be uttered again in public without mention of this indictment. If he died thirty years from now, his obituary would mention this indictment.

When he finally dragged his eyes from the documents to look at her, she said, "Bruce, there are options."

"Options?" asked Bruce.

"A deal," said Sidney. "A plea agreement." Despite all the things he had done, she wanted no part in executing him or anyone else. She didn't believe in the death penalty. Life or death was a decision for a higher power. Besides, she felt badly for his wife. Melissa had always been the one to buzz Sidney up to their condominium in the luxury eight-story Dakota Apartment building. Sidney had seen sympathy in her wide brown eyes whenever Sidney dropped off legal documents at all hours of the day, night, and weekend. His wife had wavy brunette hair, a pert nose, and usually carried a small baby on her hip. In the large apartment, which overlooked Central Park, a second child, about two years old, was frequently sprawled on a white rug, pushing a red fire truck.

"Interested?" asked Sidney.

Bruce hesitated, distracted by the motion of two men.

Even as her own brown eyes softened in sympathy, Sidney knew the FBI Deputy Director was rising from his chair. Standing guard at the door, he was soon joined by the Police Chief. In his mid-fifties, the chief was several inches shorter than Charles Thomas, with dark skin and a trim white moustache and beard. He was widely built with a thick middle, which rested on his black belt that held a black revolver and a walkie-talkie. Unlike prior Metropolitan Police Chiefs, he dressed like his men, avoiding the white uniform of ranking police officials. The breast pocket of his dark blue police uniform had the outline of a cigarette box. Sidney knew he had quit a two-pack-a-day habit ten years ago, but he still carried cigarettes in his pocket on stressful days. Earlier, she had noted his determined expression. He had been friends with the Attorney General, but she knew from experience that he was fair and would withhold judgment until the evidence was in the proper hands.

"What's the deal?" asked Drake.

"It's a winner-take-all deal."

"No deal," said Drake. "I represent three different clients here. I'm here to protect all of their interests."

"Even the two who aren't footing your bill?" asked Sidney.

Drake's face flushed as his voice rose. "Are you suggesting—"

"You bet your—"

"Hey, hey, hey," said Bruce, cutting them off. "The last time I checked, I was the only person here that got indicted today." He glared at his lawyer and then turned his full attention back to her. "What's the deal?" asked Bruce.

Sidney had worked and waited for this moment for four months. Her demeanor was poised in her tailored tan suit and matching pumps. Slender and tall, she was in her early thirties with delicate features. Four months ago, her brown eyes had been warm, her face open and honest. The man seated across from her had complimented her often on her intelligence and resourcefulness. Their working styles had meshed perfectly. During the six years she had worked as a senior associate at the law firm of Drake, Spaulding & Lloyd, he had trusted her to do a good job and she had held up her end of the bargain. However, it turned out that the joke had been on her. She had been manipulated and underestimated.

Sidney slowly crossed her legs. They were long, caramel and shapely. "As I was saying—" she looked pointedly at Drake, "the deal is winner-takes-all. We'll offer total amnesty to you if you're the first one through the door. However, if you're second, even if only by minutes, which I'm told has happened on more than one occasion, then you're subject to full prosecution." She held Bruce's gaze. "You need to understand that this offer has an expiration date."

"You need to set up a race between my clients," said Drake. "You need to break the trust between my clients."

"Trust?" spit out Bruce. "One of your *clients* threatened to hook my balls up to a car battery if I—"

"This is not the time," said Drake, holding up his hand.

Sidney ignored Drake and focused on Bruce. Sweat was dripping onto his starched white collar. His underarms were damp. She knew exactly how he felt. Four months ago, she had been sitting exactly where he was sitting. Drake was right. She intended to create tension and mistrust between his clients. Although she suspected that there was already tension and mistrust between them. She merely needed to exploit it. They would have to decide who they could trust and how much. She could see in Bruce's eyes that the race was already on. Who would be the first to provide evidence against the others? In prosecuting criminals, nothing is quite as persuasive as the testimony of an insider. Sidney had been told by the FBI Director, who was working on a major announcement, that this tactic had been responsible for winning more big cases than all of the FBI's search warrants, secret audio, or video tape interrogations combined. And she wanted to win. Four months ago, while staring into the barrel of a handgun, she had decided that this would not be over until she won.

"What do you want to know?" asked Bruce. His eyes were resigned. His small hands rested in his lap.

Sidney pursed her lips and set her elbows on the table. She could feel the air being sucked out of the room. "We want to know two things," said Sidney, holding up two fingers. "Who murdered Clay Eldridge?" She lowered one finger. "And who was the drug connection behind the murder?" She lowered the second finger.

"You think drugs were behind the murder of the Attorney General?" asked Drake, glancing at his client.

Sidney never took her eyes off Bruce. "All we need is one material witness. One insider."

"No," said Bruce Lewis.

Deputy Director Thomas tapped on the inside of the brown door of the conference room. The door opened from the other side. FBI agents, in black uniforms with yellow vests, appeared in the doorway. The door shut behind them as they entered the room and circled the table. "Bruce Lewis, you're under arrest," said Thomas. "You have the right to remain silent. Anything you say can and will be used against you in a court of law . . ."

Looking shocked, Bruce Lewis's eyes hunted the room for help. When he found none, he hung his head as his rights were read. The agents circled the table, pulled him to his feet, and handcuffed his hands behind his back. The metal clinked in the silent room. The young lawyers in the room gaped as Bruce looked at Sidney in desperation. "Please, Sidney," his bluish-gray eyes pleaded.

"There's nothing I can do," said Sidney, lowering her gaze. She had not wanted it to come to this. This summer, standing side by side in the courtroom, they had both watched in horror as Alexander shot himself.

Surrounded by agents, Bruce was led out of the room in handcuffs. As the door opened, she saw him come face to face with Roger Alexander. The two men glared at each other across the outer office. She could see the hatred and fear in their eyes. She watched Bruce's eyes pass over Alexander's scarred face and florescent orange prison jumpsuit. The navy blue suit was gone and his wrist and ankles were wrapped in iron manacles. They clanked as Alexander shuffled forward in the outer office, nudged along by a cadre of FBI agents and local police. The door to the conference room closed.

As Sidney turned, Nathaniel Drake stood up to leave. He raised his hand to his temple and mumbled something unintelligible. His full team of young lawyers stood, appearing dazed and confused.

Sidney understood his problems. She knew that he had been accustomed to winning, at least, until last winter. Like his uncle and grandfather, he had degrees from Princeton and Yale Law School. Like them, he had joined the pristine white-shoe firm of Drake, Spaulding & Lloyd, which had been founded by one of their ancestors in the 1600s. Through the midtown law firm, they had wielded tremendous influence in New York City. Then suddenly, his uncle was ensnared in an ugly scandal and was currently doing time in a minimum-security prison in Connecticut. His grandfather had dropped dead from the stress and humiliation. The firm had barely survived. He was probably wondering, "How in the hell had everything gone so wrong so fast?" Now Roger Alexander, the firm's highest profile client, was about to be executed. Moreover, one of their partners had just been indicted and arrested. Sidney really did understand his problems. She also understood that his problems were only going to get worse. She had spent many long days and nights planning it just that way.

"We have another matter," said Sidney, stopping him in his tracks.

Drake had been rounding the table when he stopped and glanced down at her. "Can this day get any worse?"

"Yes," said Sidney as her team smiled knowingly.

Drake smirked and cocked his head. "That's not possible."

"You're also representing Christina Savant?" asked Sidney. "She's one of your three clients?"

"We'll see after today," said Drake.

"Then you should know we've empanelled a special grand jury," said Sidney.

"And?"

"And her company is the target."

———————————

After a ten-minute break, Sidney heard the expected knock at the conference room door. Led by FBI agents, Roger Alexander shuffled into the room. Metal clinked.

His small eye swept over the room. "To what do I owe this pleasure?" asked Alexander.

"Have a seat," said Sidney, looking at his scarred face.

Alexander shuffled across the room and sat in a chair next to his attorney. He faced Sidney. "What do you want?"

"I have everything I want," said Sidney. "What do you want?" Sidney knew that Alexander was studying the face of the woman who had defeated him. She and her new boss were about to ascend to a position that Alexander had literally killed for.

"I want to be the United States Attorney General, can you make that happen?" asked Alexander.

"No. But the President can commute your death sentence."

Surprised, both Roger Alexander and his lawyer leaned forward. "What do you want?" asked Alexander. His tongue slid over his thin lips.

"Just a minute, Roger," said his Drake, holding up his hand. "First, we have to ensure—"

"Shut up," said Alexander, without turning his wide face. He held Sidney's gaze. "What do you want?"

"Your drug connection." Sidney glanced down the table at the head of the Drug Enforcement Agency and looked back. "And a confession to Clay Eldridge's murder." She followed Alexander's eye as it swept over the FBI-DEA Task Force. She knew he recognized most of the faces in the room. However, she was dying to peek at Drake, who she suspected was in a slow boil, but she refused to take her eyes off Alexander.

"For all of that," said Alexander, "you would commute my death sentence to life in prison?" He leaned back in his chair.

"Getting executed is serious business," said Sidney.

"So is hanging from a bed sheet in a prison cell," said Alexander. One of his former colleagues had found himself in just that predicament. "What did you offer Bruce Lewis?"

"Good luck on death row," said Sidney Cox, gathering her papers. Her team began pushing back their chairs, collecting papers and pens. The only sound in the room was the scraping of chairs on the floor.

Taken aback, Roger Alexander turned, looked at his lawyer, and then stood up. "Can't we talk about this?" Metal clanked.

"Your time is up," said Sidney, walking out the door. The last time she seen him without handcuffs, he was pointing a pistol at her. She remembered how the blood had pulsed through her veins. Time had slowed; details became vivid. She recalled the faint scent of her lawyer's cologne as he moved to protect her. She remembered the slight swing of the pistol's barrel, the gun's explosion. She had expected a bullet to rip through her flesh. Instead, blood had shot out of the chest of Peter Savant. He had slumped forward and fallen over a courtroom bench. Her hands had been shaking as the courtroom burst into pandemonium. She heard the judge pounding her gavel as she stared down at the bleeding body. Screams and shouts had become distant background noise. She had not shared with anyone how shaken she was. But, she was getting stronger day by day and sitting in court this morning had strengthened her. She had met Alexander's stare when he had scanned the courtroom. Her eyes had bore into his small eye. She was now the pursuer.

FBI agents entered the room and escorted Alexander to the door. When he reached the doorway, he stopped and stared into the outer office. Striding toward them was a woman with an erect posture and a swing to her hips. Fiery red tresses hung past her shoulders; dark emerald eyes adorned her oval face. A scarlet suit clung to her lean body. The skirt was thigh high with a slit up the side. Three-inch heels clinked on the linoleum floor as she crossed the outer office.

When she reached them, Alexander's small eye meandered down her full chest, slim hips and toned calves. He then met the

steady gaze of Christina Savant. He had not seen her since the day
he shot her brother in the courtroom downstairs.

"How are you?" asked Alexander.

"Free," said Christina. "And you?"

He shrugged his thick shoulders. "You live, you learn, you're
put to death," said Alexander. He leaned close to her ear and
whispered, "I saw you."

"I see you, too," said Christina, speaking with a faint French
accent.

"No, I saw you," he repeated. He looked at her meaningfully.
He saw her blink twice. "That's what I thought." A small smile
crossed his lips. Then he was shoved forward through the outer
office and out the door by Thomas and Police Chief Warden. Arched
eyebrows gathered, Christina watched Alexander leave.

"Come in," said Sidney, leaning against the door jamb.

Christina turned, scanned Sidney from foot to head and then
entered the conference room. Fragrant perfume trailed in her wake.
Christina gazed at Nathaniel Drake, who was seated on the other
side of the table. "I saw Bruce Lewis down the hall," she said to her
lawyer without preamble.

All eyes in the room were on her.

"He was in handcuffs," she said.

"He's under arrest," said Drake.

"And Roger Alexander received the death penalty," she said.

"This morning," said Drake.

"In that case, you're fired," she said.

Drake sank against his seat. "This is not happening to me."
He looked up at his firm's biggest client—former biggest client.
"Can we talk about this outside?"

"Why?"

"You signed a joint defense agreement," he said. "It's best if
you work together with us—and Bruce and Roger."

"So you said."

"Don't do something you'll regret," said Drake.

"Too late for that," said Christina, still standing near the door.
She watched Drake stand, and collect his papers and his troops.

He stopped near her. "I'd like you to reconsider."

"All right," she said pleasantly.

"Really?"

"No," said Christina.

He sputtered some reply that Sidney couldn't quite make out. His neck was flushed red. Sidney knew he had never been toyed with like this, especially in front of his associates. A junior associate, who had worked with his uncle, had been on the receiving end of an airborne telephone. He had been clocked in the head over a misplaced comma.

"Oh, have a seat and stop babbling," said Christina. She glanced around the room as he, and his minions, sat back down. She sat next to him. "Who's in charge here?" asked Christina.

Standing near the door, Sidney said, "How badly do you want to keep CSC?" Sidney sat down. "Your newly inherited empire?"

Christina narrowed her eyes. "You mean because Roger Alexander and his lawyer—" she looked pointedly at Drake, "implicated my company during his murder trial. After he shot my brother in your halls of justice?"

After reading her FBI file, Sidney had not been sure what to expect from Christina Savant. However, she had expected Christina to inherit her brother's company. He had died a self-made millionaire with offices around the world, including Savant Plaza, a thirty-five story silver skyscraper on Park Avenue in Manhattan. He had also died intestate—without a will—and with only one living relative. Sidney had known this even before reading the file. CSC had been her major client while she was an associate at Drake, Spaulding & Lloyd. It was the major reason why she was heading up this investigation. However, it did not hurt that she had degrees from Howard University and Yale Law School, framed but not hung, in her office; that she was well-traveled; and fluent in two languages.

"Were you—" started Sidney.

"What's with all these questions?" asked Christina, locking eyes with the dark-haired woman seated behind Sidney. "Why don't you just shine a light in my eyes?"

"Your stock is in a death spiral," said Sidney. "If we bring RICO charges against your company for laundering drug money, what will you sell first? Your private jet?"

Looking directly at Sidney, Christina relaxed her narrow shoulders. "How can I help?" she asked pleasantly.

Sidney glanced at Drake, but his thin lips were pressed shut. "We need dates, times, drug shipments."

"And I assume you can provide some level of protection for me," said Christina, "after I provide you with this information."

"Yes, we can—"

The crack of a single rifle shot pieced the morning air.

THE MONKEY IN THE WRENCH

CHAPTER 3

Ten minutes earlier. A black van backed up a paved driveway on the side of the courthouse, a six-story white limestone building engraved E. Barrett Prettyman U.S. Court House, and named for a former Chief Justice. High above, American flags whipped in the cool breeze. Men piled out of the van at twelve noon sharp. While they waited for the wide, neutral-colored garage door to rise, they glanced to the left, toward Constitution Avenue. Metropolitan police cars, with engines running, waited on Constitution Avenue and, behind them, on Third Street, between the courthouse and the Department of Labor.

In front of the courthouse, reporters and camera crews crowded onto the front concrete plaza. Restrained by blue police barricades, they trampled the lush green grass surrounding the pavement, jockeying for a better position. The agents had been warned that the media would be waiting by the front exit. According to the Deputy Director's analysis, nearly two thousand journalists had descended upon the District. Thomas had wanted them to be prepared for anything. He had conducted multi-district strategy sessions with the FBI and the police departments from both the District and Virginia. Virginia officers were needed for the transport to and from Lynnwood, Virginia.

Hence, they had bought the prisoner up through the basement and out the side garage. Within seconds of arriving, the agents heard doors unlocking and opening in the back of the garage. The garage door rose and the prisoner appeared. Shuffling forward, he wore a black bullet-proof vest, and was surrounded by agents. He was led by Charles Thomas and Police Chief David Warden. Thomas looked skyward toward a whirring sound. In the distance, against a bluish-gray sky, he saw a news helicopter just beyond the U.S. Capitol dome.

In that instance, a single shot rang out. Roger Alexander grabbed his neck. Blood seeped through his fingers. The two agents holding his arms grasped him tighter. Alexander was breathing heavily. He couldn't catch his breath. His hand clutched his chest, giving the impression that he felt it might explode. His skin turned clammy and cold. He staggered forward and crumpled to the ground. Holding him tightly, the two agents fell to their knees on the pavement.

"Get down," shouted Thomas, as he dragged the Police Chief down. The pavement was cool and hard.

Semi-automatic fire swept over their heads. There were shouts as agents hit the deck. District police cars hit their sirens. Blue and white lights whirled. Police cars swarmed up the driveway, shielding the agents with their vehicles. Weapons were drawn and officers took cover behind the vehicles. New police cars arrived from all directions.

Crouched behind a police car, Thomas glimpsed a Virginia police medallion on an arriving police car. They were two minutes late. He glanced around, looking for injuries. He saw none. Police Chief Warden was squatting next to him. Warden appeared surprised, but unharmed. As Thomas turned his head, the sharpshooter's rifle glistened in the sun from a nearby rooftop. Thomas glimpsed a heavy, stainless steel barrel of a M24 SWS. Used by SWAT teams, it was designed for the United States military. His brow creased. Two seconds passed and the Remington vanished, replaced by the sniper dismantling a bipod, the mounted scope and the weapon, and inserting them in a carrying case. Within two more seconds, he disappeared.

Pointing across the street, toward the Department of Labor, Thomas shouted, "The shooter is on the rooftop. He's wearing all black—black boots and black headgear. He has a M24 SWS Remington rifle, with a mounted Leupold Mark IV M3 scope, in a black carrying case." Thomas motioned specific agents to give chase. Police cars began backing out, but blocked in by Virginia police cars, they were slow to pull out. Officers were waving and shouting. Chief Warden stepped in with specific directions to his men. Thomas motioned for other officers to move out on foot, crossing Third Street, heading toward the large federal building. He sent others to block off reporters, who were rushing toward them. He had his top agents contain the prisoner.

Striding toward Alexander, Thomas kneeled down and pressed two fingers against his neck. Thomas felt warm sticky blood, but no pulse. The blood was bright red and spurting onto the pavement. "Damn," he said. He pressed his fingers harder against the thick neck. He felt a very faint pulse. Thomas exhaled and then Alexander's eye rolled back in his head. "Call the paramedics!" Thomas shouted as he stood. Around him, there was total chaos. FBI agents, as well as District and Virginia police, were moving in all directions. "Did someone call for an ambulance?" shouted Thomas.

"Yes," said Chief Warden, returning to his side.

"Thanks, man," said Thomas. Turning to one of his agents, he said, "Get these Virginia police cars out of here. And have our agents work with Chief Warden to move his men out in a six-block radius. I want this area isolated in under sixty seconds. I want that sharpshooter caught now."

As they hurried away, an ambulance siren pierced the racket. Police cars moved to let it through. It swerved around blocked cars. Wearing black jackets and stethoscopes, three young paramedics jumped out of the ambulance as it slowed. Carrying a red gurney and equipment, they moved efficiently through the crowd. Directed by Thomas, they rushed to Alexander's side. He was laying face down on the cement.

A paramedic spoke into a walkie-talkie. "Unit five, we're at the scene." Checking the prisoner's pulse, he said, "Weak pulse, no respiration. He's still alive, but just barely." He looked at the inmate closely. "It's a GSW?"

"Yes, it's a gunshot wound," said Thomas.

The paramedics leaned closer. Bright red blood flowed. Arterial bleeding—bleeding from the artery—spurted bright red blood. Bleeding from a vein would have been a darker red color and would have oozed out. "Looks like he's been shot in his carotid artery." Wearing plastic gloves, they carefully turned him onto his back. His eye rolled from the back of his head and stared straight ahead. They lowered his eyelid and his face fell to the side.

Thomas inhaled. Alexander had been shot in the neck, in the main artery supplying blood to his brain. It could only be worse if he had been shot in the jugular vein, which was nearby. From his training, Thomas knew that when a major artery was severed, blood could spurt up four meters and a person could die within two minutes. However, he also knew that an adult body held up to six liters of blood and could lose up to three liters before his life would be in danger. He watched the paramedics apply direct pressure on the wound with a pad of bandages. They elevated Alexander by raising his head and placing his arm over a paramedic's shoulder to slow the bleeding. Moving Alexander as little as possible, they inserted a white plastic tube into his mouth.

Thomas scanned the area as some of his agents returned. "Anything? Anybody see the shooter?" The agents replied with blank stares and shrugged shoulders.

It doesn't look good," said one of the paramedics finally. "We're not getting a BP, so we're going to start an IV." A second paramedic prepared the IV and pulled up Alexander's sleeve. After he finished, Alexander's pupil stayed fixed and dilated. They attached him to an ECG monitor. They waited. No reaction. They tried again. Time ticked by. "There's no heart tone and no carotid pulse." There was no sign of life. The paramedic looked up at Thomas.

He nodded.

"What time is it?" asked a paramedic. "Let the coroner know we've pronounced Roger Alexander dead at twelve eighteen in the afternoon. Does he have a donor card?"

"I don't know," said Thomas.

As they covered Alexander with a white sheet, a paramedic said, "Call the dispatch center, give them the time of death, and get a case number." The paramedic placed a hospital-type band around Alexander's right ankle.

Thomas knew the band would later contain the case number; the paramedic's identification number; and the time and date of death. The case number would later be used to identify the body for a death certificate. As they placed his body on the gurney and strapped him in, Thomas glanced up at the helicopter overhead. The sharp blades were cutting into the wind. He noticed the news logo on the helicopter. When he looked back down, the paramedics were lifting his prisoner's body into the back of the ambulance.

"Damn, damn, damn," muttered Thomas. "Stop." The paramedics turned as he strode to the ambulance and pressed two fingers against inmate's neck and then to his wrist. Thomas frowned. "Proceed," he said. He turned to his lieutenant. "Go with them," he said.

"No, I'll go," said Police Chief Warden, stepping forward.

"That's not necessary, David," said Thomas.

"This happened in my city. It's necessary," said David Warden, walking toward the ambulance.

Standing in the driveway, Thomas watched his friend catch up with the paramedics and jostle into the back of the ambulance. He heard one of the paramedics mutter something in Spanish. The ambulance and remaining police cars pulled away. Standing in the middle of the chaos, Thomas looked up at the sky, raised his arms and then let them fall to his side in frustration.

———

Wednesday at 1 P.M. Less than one hour later, Sidney Cox and Charles Thomas entered a conference room in the Department of Justice. They sat at the head of a long mahogany table. Around the table, expressions ranged from apprehensive to expectant. At the front of the room, near the vaulted ceiling, a golden eagle on the Great Seal watched over the Task Force.

Sidney flipped open a small, black, three-ring binder notebook.

"We have two problems," said Sidney. "Alexander never arrived at any hospital or any morgue in the District of Columbia, Virginia or even Maryland." A murmur arose. She waited for it to die down. "And David Warden has disappeared." Hurt filled her eyes. Without glancing at Thomas, she knew he felt worse. "The Police Chief left with the ambulance and has not been heard from since."

Thomas blinked twice. "Also, even though a lot of shots were fired, we found only one shell and no bullets."

"I don't understand," said the head of the Drug Enforcement Agency.

"It gets worse." Thomas looked at him thoughtfully. "The real Virginia police arrived late. The plan was twelve noon sharp. What appeared to be Virginia police cars arrived two minutes after twelve. I spoke with the Virginia police captain. A little after eleven thirty this morning, he received a call. He was asked to delay his units' arrival by thirty minutes. He was told that the meeting with Roger Alexander was running over. And that we didn't want to tip off the media to our transport plan."

"They took the word of an anonymous caller?" asked Paul Martinez, the DEA head. As he leaned forward, he ran his hand through his dark hair. Fortyish, he had light brown skin and was clean shaven. He was a career DEA agent responsible for several major drug busts before the President appointed him to head the agency. If things went well, he would advance to the Deputy Director position when Thomas was promoted. However, things were not going well.

Setting his elbows on the table, Thomas pressed his fingertips together. "The caller knew the police captain's private office number and our code name for the prison transport," said Thomas.

"Who had that information?" asked a female voice from the doorway. As the faces in the room turned, Wendy Shannon entered the room through large brown double doors. The U.S. Attorney for the District of Columbia was flanked by several of her investigators. She was a short, tough, fortyish blonde with wide hips and gray eyes. Her skin was weathered from years of tanning, smoking and drinking vodka. She wore a crisp suit with an expensive matte gold necklace. Apparently, she had been watching the news. "Well, Charles?" said Shannon, pressing her round-rimmed glasses up her nose.

They stared at each other in silence.

For ten years, Wendy Shannon had worked in this building. During most of that time, she had slaved away in abject obscurity in the Public Integrity Section of the Justice Department. But, in rapid succession, she had prosecuted four corrupt federal judges. Impressed by her success, her former boss had handpicked her to investigate the Speaker of the U.S. House of Representatives. Working non-stop for months with five career prosecutors and ten FBI agents, she successfully charged, prosecuted and jailed the Speaker for income tax evasion. Page-one recognition in the *Washington Post* followed. She used her newfound prestige to stab her boss in the back. Within two months, she had his job. Within days of President Wright's election, she was in the Oval Office lobbying for an appointment as the new U.S. Attorney for the District of Columbia. In her new position, she controlled the largest federal prosecution office in the country. She now managed 600 people, oversaw 21 different law enforcement agencies, and reported directly to the Attorney General.

Unfortunately, he was currently dead and the man who had been nominated for the post, the current FBI Director, was not her biggest fan. She had made a number of mistakes that had blown up in his face. However, she knew that the FBI Director admired the integrity of the man staring back at her. Charles Thomas had proven to be circumspect and tightlipped about agency business. After a clean bust in a sprawling political corruption case in New York City, the Director had promoted Thomas to Deputy Director to help him supervise 56 FBI field offices and 400 satellite offices scattered around the country.

"Did I miss a meeting?" asked Shannon.

Sidney exhaled. "Wendy, why don't you have seat?" It was obvious Shannon felt she had redeemed herself with the conviction of Roger Alexander.

Shannon cocked her head and then motioned for her

investigators to take seats at the other end of the table. She sat between them. On the east wall, over Shannon's head, was an abhorrent mural entitled *Justice Denied*. Painted during the 1930s, the mural displayed a satanic man holding an angelic mask. Common people are being mugged and lashed in a barren landscape. On the opposite end, at Sidney's back, was a companion mural entitled *Justice Triumphs*. The judge clutched a law book. Common people climbed to higher ground, to fertile fields. A woman draped in white held up two fingers. She was truth personified.

"Who had the prison transport code?" asked Shannon, locking eyes with Thomas.

"That's what we're working on," said Sidney.

"What about the paramedics?" asked Wendy Shannon.

"They weren't real," offered Sidney.

"The real ambulance arrived moments later," said Thomas. "The one that we called for."

"Who arranged for the first one?" asked Shannon.

"We don't know yet," said Thomas.

"What do you know?" asked Shannon.

The electricity between them sizzled.

Sidney glanced from one to the other. She couldn't read the expression on Shannon's face. However, since there was no love lost between Shannon and herself, and Sidney had bigger fish to fry, she let it drop for now. The brown double doors to the room opened and a staffer walked into the room. Her long dark hair fell forward as she handed a brown folder to Sidney. Sidney pulled the document out, scanned it and signed the extradition order. When the staffer left the room, Sidney said, "We've obtained film from one of the networks. They had a helicopter in the air. Let's start there."

On Sidney's cue, the lights went off in the conference room. As the attendees blinked against the darkness, a white screen descended from the ceiling. Within seconds, they watched Roger Alexander come to life in Technicolor and surround sound.

Thomas stood and walked to the screen, with a pointer. The action on screen paused at intervals as he pointed. "This is the single shot that dropped Alexander," he said. "However, there were more shots." On the screen, Thomas dropped to his knees, dragging Chief Warden with him. "Multiple semi-automatic shots, but not one injury. Except to Alexander." The action on screen proceeded and then paused. Thomas pointed to the blood on the white paved driveway. "See this blood?"

"What about it?" said Shannon. "It's not that much."

"That's my point," said Thomas. "There's not enough blood here for the kind of injuries sustained by Alexander." The lights came up. The white screen ascended into the ceiling. Thomas laid down pointer. "We believe blanks were fired. That the only shot fired was the first shot. The question is 'Why?'"

Wednesday at midnight. Twelve hours later, the man opened his eye. It shifted, straining to focus. Images were blurry. His head ached and his mouth was dry. If he was in hell, it really was hot and steamy, he thought. He ran his tongue over his thin lips. He tried to lift a heavy hand to his pale face. His hand fell back to his side. It fell on something soft, something he was lying on. He shifted his hips. It felt like he was lying on a cot. He closed his eye and then opened it again. It roamed down over the florescent orange jumpsuit that he was wearing. A face leaned into view. He focused on it. The image began to clear. Dark eyes, ginger skin, neatly trimmed dark hair, expensive black suit, and striped tie.

Roger Alexander tried to raise his head. It was heavy and painful. "What a day," mumbled Alexander.

"I'll say," said the voice, with a Spanish accent.

"I was sentenced to die." Alexander leaned on one arm and glared at the man who was squatting next to the cot. "And then you executed me."

"Actually, I resurrected you."

"Actually," said Alexander, "you've put me on the FBI's Ten Most Wanted List."

"Join the club."

Alexander struggled to sit up. He felt the other man's firm hand on his arm, pulling him into a sitting position. Alexander looked down and then turned his head. He was lying on a cot in the middle of a long, narrow building with a concrete floor and iron roof. It was a large open space with hundreds of sweaty young men and women, barely dressed, seated on long benches at rows and rows of tables. They packed white powder into clear plastic packets. Two women entering were subjected to body frisks and bag searches. At the other end was a fully equipped chemistry laboratory. As he turned back, Alexander clutched his neck. "Jesus, that stings. What did you shoot me with?"

"A special brew," said Andres Santos, smiling.

Alexander frowned. "Not with any of this stuff?" he asked, nodding his head toward the lab.

"When you feel up to it, let's chat," he said, standing. "Then I have something to show you."

"What now?"

"Where are the records?"

Alexander rubbed his sore wrists. The chains were gone from his wrists and ankles. "What do you want to show me?" asked Alexander.

"That depends on what you have to say about the financial records."

They heard a commotion at the door. A presence entered the room like a Tasmanian devil, noisy and spirited. The young woman wore white leather pants and a cropped red top. Petite, her abs were tight, her jet-black hair styled short. Two years younger, she was a female version of Andres.

"What are you doing here?" asked Andres. His dark eyes glanced over his younger sister. "And what the hell are you wearing?"

"We have bigger issues than my attire," said his sister.

"What's the problem?" asked Andres.

"An extradition order was signed today," she said.

They both turned, looking intently at Alexander sitting on the cot. Alexander closed his eye. The siblings nodded in unison and five armed men immediately surrounded Alexander.

"Oh, for the love of God," said Alexander, falling back on the cot. "Will this day never end?"

Five minutes later, Andres Santos was driving a black Jeep Cherokee through thick underbrush. Next to him, Alexander brooded in silence. Soft white moonlight filtered through a rustic canopy of leaves springing from massive trees. Straining in the dark, his small eye took in every passing tree, branch and bark. He watched for landmarks as Andres's men huddled in the back of the Jeep. They were heavily armed and most of their weapons were pointed at Alexander's head.

"Are you worn out from your flight?" asked Andres.

"Those twelve-hour, red-eye flights from the States to Colombia usually pucker me out," said Alexander. "That and being shot."

"Sorry about that," said Andres.

"I thought you were bringing some real power to this task," said Alexander, as the humid air clung to his skin. The jumpsuit began to hang heavily from his body. "Like some machine guns."

"Finesse, my friend."

"What about my plastic surgery?" demanded Alexander, watching the headlights of the jeep cut through the dense forest. "That was part of the deal."

Andres braked and turned off the engine, leaving on the headlights. "We're here."

"Where the hell is 'here'?" asked Alexander, glancing around. There was dense vegetation covering the ground. There were vines and colorful flora. There were weird insects buzzing around. But there was no 'here.'

"Get out," said Andres.

"No," says Alexander.

Andres pointed a .38-caliber pistol at Alexander's head.

"That's been happening a lot lately," said Alexander. He studied Andres's grim expression. He heard weapons lock and load behind him. He stepped out of the Jeep. His feet slid into the thick undergrowth. The air was thick with sweet scents.

"What's next?" asked Alexander.

"You know the drill," said Andres.

Frowning, Alexander walked away from the vehicle, up a mound. He turned his head slightly.

"Stop right there," said Andres.

"Are you planning to stab me in the back?" asked Alexander. "And mind you, for most people, that's merely a figure of speech."

"No, I intend to shoot you."

"Would you prefer to shoot me in the back or between the eyes?" asked Alexander, without turning.

"Since you only have the one eye," said Andres, "I'll opt for a single shot through the heart." Andres stepped out of the jeep. The other men followed. "Turn around."

"There's other evidence against you," said Alexander, without turning. He thought about his meeting with Sidney Cox. He had been surprised when she had not mentioned his laptop. The FBI Director had had a firm grip on it when Alexander pulled the trigger in the courthouse. "I can help you find it before the others do."

"What others?"

Alexander turned to face him.

They heard choppers slicing the air in the distance. Through the thick overhead leaves, they glimpsed an army of helicopters heading their way. Intense bluish-white lights streamed through the branches and leaves. They all ducked for cover. Andres crept around the jeep and switched off the headlights. His dark eyes tracked the helicopters. After several minutes, they passed overhead. He turned his attention back to Alexander. Alexander was gone. The place where he had been standing was empty. Andres jumped up, scanning the area. His men did likewise. Turning in a full circle, he caught a glimpse of the florescent orange jumpsuit moving speedily through the woods. He heard the helicopters circle back. He glanced up and saw them descend on the large narrow building. His jaw went slack.

"What about Alexander?" asked one of his men.

"What about my sister?" asked Andres.

"What about us?" asked another man.

Standing in the middle of the chaos, Andres looked up at the sky, raised his arms and then let them fall to his side in frustration.

Alexander lumbered through the woods at full speed. Branches lashed his arms and back. His shoe caught in the underbrush. He stumbled, but managed to stay upright. Although his mind was still foggy from whatever he had been shot with, his eye hunted through the gloom for any of the landmarks he had seen earlier. *Which way should he go?* he wondered. Everything appeared the same—green or brown, and lush. He heard helicopter blades whipping in the wind overhead. He glanced up into a stream of bright lights. He leapt to his right. Were those voices behind him? He heard the engine of the black jeep start. He ran harder. He heard machine gun fire in the distance. He began panting and perspiration gushed from his pores. He had made mistakes, but good god, how had it come to this? Sweat poured from his body, making the jumpsuit cling to his broad, middle-aged body. His lungs burned. His foot caught on a thick vine. He went down. He crashed face first into the soft ground. This was the second time today. This morning he had gone down into cement. His face hurt. He lay there, exhausted, taking deep breaths. The rich scent of plants and moist ground filled his senses. He wondered what would happen if he decided not to move, ever again, just lay there in the vines and vegetation. Then something crawled over his hand.

"Damn." He sat up, shaking his hand. He put his hand to his forehead. "What else can possibly go wrong?" sighed Alexander. After a minute, he stood up, brushing leaves and dirt from his jumpsuit when a big gray bag dropped over his head. He was in complete darkness. He could feel his warm breath against his face. He threw punches, fighting the bag and stumbling about. His screams were muffled by the bag. He tried to run, but he couldn't see a thing. He ran smack into a tree. "What the hell?!" He struggled against the soft bag. He stumbled and fell. He felt strong hands pulling the bag down over his thick shoulders, down his waist and legs. Hands and sharp elbows pressed against him, wrapping him in the bag.

Until now, Alexander had won all the major battles in his life. The first was with his mother. He was in the fourth grade when his mother decided to send him to therapy. She was an outgoing and brilliant woman whose authority he constantly thwarted. She would call him down to breakfast from his room above the attic. He was consistent in his response—hostile silence. One day, he had heard her footsteps on the stairs, but refused to move from his position across the bed. Out of breath, her chest heaved as she stepped into the room. As she fought for calm, she stared at the hockey paraphernalia covering all four walls. Hockey sticks were in one corner, leaning against the wall. He recalled she was wearing a long white apron over a red ginger dress as the argument descended into a two-way, two-hour verbal bloodletting. He had felt an adrenaline rush. Although his mother had been strong-willed, she and the counselor had finally concluded, after years of battling, that he could not be beaten. She would just have to adjust.

Now he was completely wrapped up in a bag in the middle of some jungle. He fought hard, but he was growing weak. Just when he was about to give up, he felt the hands and elbows pull away. Flailing around in the bag, Alexander eventually got to his feet. He heard a spark and a crackle of electricity. His muscles constricted as he was suddenly hit by a volt of electricity. He pitched forward, slamming into the ground. "God dammit." Even in his haze, he wondered why someone didn't just shoot him and put him out of his misery.

"Hello, my lovely," said a sexy feminine voice.

Alexander tried to rise.

"If you lie very still, I won't hit you with two hundred and fifty thousand volts of electricity again."

Alexander lay very still. Was that tangy scent his own burning flesh? he wondered. After several minutes passed, he felt the bag being pulled over his shoulders and head. His eye searched the faces around him. It paused. His eyebrow rose in confusion and then his face contorted in anger. He tried to sit up.

"You have seven lives left," she said. "Use them wisely."

Dazed, Alexander dropped to his elbow and stared up at the stun gun. It was a small one with a 9-volt nickel cadmium rechargeable battery.

"They say," she said, "it won't cause permanent damage. Just disrupt your neural and muscular system, immobilizing you. But I can tell from the look on your face, it must be causing some mental confusion because you're still looking mighty brave." She placed a finger on the trigger. "But I only inquired about a five-second burst. Shall we see what happens with a ten-second jolt?"

He lay back down.

"No?"

"They'll figure this out," he said.

"They think you're already dead."

THE HAVE NOTS

———————

CHAPTER 4

Thursday morning. "We don't think he's dead," said Sidney Cox. She surveyed the surprised faces in the Justice Department conference room.

"Roger Alexander is alive?" asked Wendy Shannon, the U.S. Attorney.

"What about a pulse?" asked one of the agents. "I saw you check for one." Perplexed, he looked at Deputy Director Thomas. "There wasn't one."

"We don't know why there was a faint pulse and then no pulse," said Thomas. "Maybe it had something to do with the shot. Or maybe with the IV administered by the paramedics."

"We also don't know if Alexander is still alive," said Sidney. "Did he escape or was he kidnapped?"

"When will we know?" asked Shannon.

A female staffer entered the room and handed a report to Sidney. The staffer sat down next to Sidney. Sidney flipped it open and scanned it. She passed the report to Thomas who examined it.

"Well?" asked Shannon, tapping a pen on the mahogany table.

"Alexander didn't have a pulse," said Sidney, "because he was shot with a tranquilizer."

"A tranquilizer?" asked Paul Martinez, the DEA head.

Sidney watched Thomas set the report down. "We had the FBI lab run a test on Alexander's blood," she said. "They found a strong sedative."

"What kind?" asked Martinez.

"Medetomidine mixed with ketamine," said Sidney.

"What's that?"

"An animal sedative," said Thomas. "Mostly for horses and lions. According to this report," he read from it, "it decreases cardiac output. It also causes prolonged hypotension, respiratory depression, hyperglycemia, and thermoregulatory controlled depression." Thomas looked up at blank stares. "In other words, hardly any pulse. Hardly any heartbeat. Hardly any breathing. A lot of sugar in the blood and a low body temperature." Had a Jack Ruby-type-gunman done something with Alexander?

"That explains why Charles couldn't find a pulse," said Sidney.

"Did it kill him?" asked Shannon, stopping her pen.

An hour later, the Task Force reconvened in the conference room. Sidney said, "We've instituted a global manhunt for Roger Alexander."

"Sidney and I have just spoken with President Wright and the FBI Director," said Charles Thomas. "We've been authorized to put Roger Alexander on the FBI's Ten Most Wanted List."

It was not easy to make the list. Nearly six thousand qualified candidates were winnowed down to a tidy ten. However, this was a big case. The media was salivating. Roger Alexander, the Deputy Attorney General, had killed Peter Savant, business tycoon and CEO of CSC. As one of the President's largest campaign contributors, Peter Savant, as well as the Vice President and his wife, had pushed for Alexander's appointment. Speculation about political corruption would soon be boiling.

"Where is your boss?" asked Shannon.

"The Director is testifying before a House-Senate Joint committee," said Sidney. She knew the meeting was behind closed, soundproof doors on the top floor of the nation's capitol. She had briefed him for the session. She had quickly realized this had been a professional job. It had taken someone under eighteen minutes to snatch a convicted felon from the FBI.

"Shouldn't he be here?" asked Shannon. "Are they grilling him on how we lost our star witness in the murder case of the millennium?" She glanced at Thomas.

When Sidney saw Thomas set his jaw, she said, "Deputy Director Thomas has already contacted all fourteen intelligence agencies in Washington, including the FBI, the CIA, NSA, as well as the Department for Homeland Security. Each of the FBI's fifty-six field offices, four hundred satellite offices, forty foreign offices and twelve thousand special agents are already on high alert. He's notified the border patrols, the coast guard, the FAA, and Interpol. And his staff is currently getting in touch with all U.S. embassies through the State Department."

"And DEA stands ready to provide whatever assistance Charles needs," said Paul Martinez, looking at Shannon. "At his request, we've already alerted our ten thousand employees and seventy-eight foreign offices. Moreover, DEA Air Wing is on stand by." DEA Air Wing provided sophisticated electronic, air-based assistance to federal, state, and local law enforcement agencies. It was a key component of DEA's two-billion dollar annual budget.

"We've also placed all the airports, train stations, and bus stations on high alert," added Sidney. "Roger Alexander's mug shot circled the globe in the last fifteen minutes. With a two-million dollar reward on his head."

Everyone turned to face Wendy Shannon.

She frowned and then switched focus. "I thought we already had ten fugitives," said Shannon, "on the FBI's Most Wanted List."

"As of last night," said Sidney, "we have an opening."

––––––––

"Where is my sister?" asked Andres Santos. He was standing in the middle of his living room in Bogotá, Colombia. It was tastefully decorated with antique furniture and dramatic paintings of scarlet and indigo.

His men looked from one to the other. "We searched what was left of the factory," said one. "DEA raided it, arrested people and then leveled it. They even irradiated the poppy crops. There's nothing left."

Andres lowered his voice. "I don't care about the crops."

Practically inseparable since childhood, he and his younger sister had traveled to America to attend Phillips Exeter Academy, a prestigious private school in Exeter, New Hampshire, founded in 1781, as the children of a prominent South American classical violist. However, that was right before their mother ran off with the local drug dealer.

"We need more men," said Andres.

"We recruited hundreds of men to search the underbrush and wooded areas for her. They've been at it for hours."

"Go back out there," said Andres, pacing the floor. This was not supposed to happen to his family, he thought. He kept a personal security detail that numbered as high as fifty men. He received threats from guerrillas, paramilitary fighters and other drug traffickers who had a large stake in the southern coca fields. And no one had successfully touched him yet.

The men moved to leave.

"Wait," said Andres. "Did you find Roger Alexander?

"No—"

"No?" Andres stopped pacing. "After everything that I did for him, that blood-sucking insect double-crossed me?"

"We've got his sister," said Thomas. He hesitated while the conference room burst into applause. Still clapping, Sidney stood up. The other members of the Task Force followed. Martinez beamed. The last one seated, Shannon, stood reluctantly.

"Operation Black Ice has been an eighteen-month investigation," said Thomas. "This is our biggest catch to date. Last night, we arrested Ana Santos of the Santos cartel. For those of you who are new to the Task Force, I'll give you a bit of background. As you know, the top priority of this administration is President Wright's zero tolerance drug program. It places the focus where it should be—on the big dealers. For small-time users, we provide drug treatment."

On Thomas's cue, the lights went down. In the darkness, a white screen descended from the ceiling. Thomas walked to the screen with a pointer. Two photos appeared, side by side. It was a man and woman. They had a similar facial structure, with black eyes and hair.

"Ana and Andres Santos manage a multi-billion dollar cartel near Bogotá, Colombia," said Thomas. "The Santos cartel smuggles hundreds of tons of cocaine, heroin and methamphetamine across our borders every year. That organization is responsible for one-third of all the cocaine consumed in the United States. It has been the DEA's number one target. So we put both Santos on the most wanted list," said Thomas. "Brother and sister are very close. They have an established division of labor. With an MBA from New York University, she manages the business aspect, including laundering the cash. He handles the crop production, product manufacturing and distribution." Unconsciously, Thomas cracked his knuckles. "But even with a two-million-dollar bounty on them, we haven't been able to touch them. Until now." He paused. On the screen behind Thomas, a satellite image of a long, narrow building appeared in a rainforest. It disappeared and was replaced by an image of a coca crop. Then a poppy crop appeared. The next three photos showed a leveled building and burned crop fields. ""Ana Santos was arrested last night, a little after midnight, Colombia time. Sidney has already signed an order seeking her extradition."

Sidney and Thomas both knew the Santos had achieved an almost mythical gangster status, running an operation that involved speed boats, jets, and secret air strips. They paid millions of dollars each year to bribe police and judges, generals and governors. They had murdered anyone who stood between them and their goal, including using a vice to crack open the head of a drug prosecutor.

A cell phone rang. Everyone in the conference room reached for briefcases, breast pockets or purses. "It's mine," said Sidney, taking the cell out of her purse. She dropped her car keys on the table. A silver, palm-sized canister of mace hung from the key ring. She glanced at the back-lit number on her phone. "I'll take it outside." She avoided the questioning glance from Thomas. During the past few months, they has shared and scrutinized each detail of this case together. "While I'm gone, perhaps you and Martinez can fill in the group on the President's agenda," said Sidney.

Thomas watched her leave, and then he and Martinez brought the group up to date. President Wright has visited Colombia, Peru, Bolivia, and Ecuador during the last four months as part of his Western Hemisphere Strategy. He had increased funding for military interdiction and to decrease human violations in the drug war. With coca cultivation greatly diminished in Peru and Bolivia, but vastly increased in Colombia, the Colombian President had vowed to launch a war without mercy against drug traffickers. This arrest will provide him with a great deal of leverage. President Wright and the FBI Director were now working on a historic strategy. It would be announced after the midterm elections next Tuesday. The President's party had been widely expected to gain seats in the House and Senate. However, his poll numbers were plummeting after the debacle with Roger Alexander. Thomas felt responsible.

The large double doors to the conference room opened. Sidney walked in, wearing a grim expression. All eyes in the room turned to her. "The white cars used as fake patrol cars were found. In a parking lot at National Airport. Virginia police medallions and roof lights were found in the car trunks. Black jackets with the red insignia patch of the closest hospital, blue police uniforms and gloves were also found. We located the car dealers where the cars were purchased. They were purchased under false names, with cash." Sidney swallowed. "There aren't any records of anyone suspicious having taken any flights out of that airport. Not anyone meeting the descriptions that we provided."

"What about prints?" asked Shannon.

"No prints." Sidney locked eyes with Thomas. "Charles, may I talk to you outside?"

"Sidney," he said, emotion passing behind his eyes. "It's important for everyone to hear this."

"If you're sure . . ." Sidney searched her friend's eyes. Charles Thomas was as responsible as anyone for her escape from death row. She waited for his silent nod. She sighed. "We found David Warden," she said. No one in the room moved. "He was found in the trunk of one of the cars. The Police Chief was shot through the heart."

———————

Moving as quickly as her cane would allow, Judge Lombard marched up the steps to her elevated brown bench. Her dim blue eyes swept her courtroom. She looked at the prosecution table. Two attorneys sat there. That was as it should be. She glanced at the defendant's table. She saw one lead attorney; a row of junior associates; and one empty chair. That was not as it should be. "Mr. Drake," said Judge Lombard, "where is your client?"

Everyone turned to stare at the lawyer. Drake looked at the judge, rose to his feet, and opened his mouth. At that moment, the double doors of the courtroom swung open. Everyone turned. Christina Savant strode up the center aisle with an alluring swing to her hips. Looking tan and fit, she moved to the front through the three-foot swinging doors. She sat down next to her lawyer and crossed her shapely legs. Nathaniel Drake looked down at the top of her red head, closed his mouth and then sat down.

"It's good of you to show up, Ms. Savant," said the Judge.

"I trust that my tardiness will not impact the outcome of this hearing," said Christina Savant with a faint French accent.

"I trust that you're on time for matters of importance to you." Blue eyes met emerald eyes. "Let's move on," said the Judge, putting on her half-glasses and studying several documents before her. "I've reviewed the legal briefs of both parties. The brief from Nathaniel Drake, counsel for Christina Savant, on behalf of CSC, including an affidavit signed by the board of directors." She glanced at the prosecution table. There was a kindly twinkle as she gazed at Sidney Cox. "I have also reviewed the brief from Sidney Cox, on behalf of the United States, as well as the sworn affidavit of Wendy Shannon, the U.S. Attorney for the District of Columbia." The twinkle faded. "I'll frame the matter at issue as I see it. Then each counsel will have two minutes, and two minutes only, to argue on behalf of their client. Any questions?"

The attorneys nodded.

"The Department of Justice has filed a motion seeking leave to file RICO charges against CSC," said the Judge. "Centennial Security Corporation is objecting to this motion. Christina Savant, the estranged half-sister of Peter Savant, inherited his interest in the company after he was shot to death in this very courtroom and died intestate. Thus, no will. Also, there were no other named heirs. However, under New York statute, Ms. Savant successfully won her suit to claim the inheritance. Now, within months of her victory, Ms. Savant finds herself under the gun as the stock price is plummeting under the scandal. And she expects that the company will crash and burn if Ms. Cox is successful in her motion before this court. CSC, and Ms. Savant by extension, would be branded criminals." Judge Lombard removed her half-glasses. "How am I doing so far?"

The attorneys nodded.

"Good," said the Judge. "Then now would be a good time to hear from the prosecution."

Sidney Cox rose to her feet. "Your Honor, the Justice Department has three quick points to make. First, we're asking for a grand jury hearing on Monday. We—"

Nathaniel Drake jumped to his feet. "Your Honor, we strongly object. We have yet to establish that these charges are even appropriate. Much less that a hearing date should be scheduled."

"If we give them more time," said Sidney, "they'll start shredding documents."

"I resent that." Drake faced Sidney. "And you can not be serious about a RICO charge." Drake felt frustrated. "We're not organized crime."

"Please have a seat, Mr. Drake," said the judge. She waited for him to take his seat. "These are very serious charges, Ms. Cox."

"We are aware of that, Your Honor," said Sidney. "We believe that criminal charges are completely appropriate under the circumstances. As you are well aware, the Racketeer—Influenced and Corrupt Organization Statute, commonly referred to as the 'RICO Statute,' became law in 1970. At that time, it was focused on organized crime. However, over the years, the statute has been expanded. Now, it's sufficiently broad to eliminate any criminal enterprise."

"CSC is a legitimate business, Your Honor," said Drake, from his seat. "RICO doesn't apply to us. We are not gangsters." His eyes were steady; his silver hair smooth.

"See Section 1961," said Sidney, "under the RICO chapter in 18 U.S.C.A. Money laundering is racketeering. A pattern thereof." She turned to Drake. "If you check the Department of Justice's Criminal Resource Manual under Section 110, you'll see that it specifically prohibits transporting narcotics over the border."

"Your Honor, we'd be subject to treble damages."

"Exactly," said Sidney. "As well as punitive damages."

"Is she trying to shut us down? We have thousands of employees. Their livelihoods depend on this company, Your Honor. We can't pay three times the amount of damages on top of some ungodly amount of money that twelve jurors think we should pay."

The judge studied him. "In that case, Mr. Drake, I suggest you write your Congresswoman because we don't rewrite the law here." She smiled. "Not usually."

"Your Honor," said Sidney, "under the RICO statute, CSC would be subjected to the jurisdiction of a single federal court. Your court. We wouldn't have to chase after them from state to state under a series of state criminal and civil statutes. And Mr. Drake knows that."

"Sidney," said Drake, "you need special circumstances to charge my client under the RICO statute."

"Murder, kidnapping, and drug dealing are special circumstances," said Sidney.

He glanced at his client. Her dark green eyes were expressionless.

Centennial Security Corporation was in the business of leasing security trucks, managing secured warehouses and leasing surveillance equipment with divisions in North America, South America, Europe and Africa. But, one of its fastest-growing divisions transferred forfeited assets—money, cars, drug paraphernalia, drugs. Anything valuable owned by drug dealers, CSC hauled it for local police departments. CSC had even had a large contract with the Justice Department.

"You Honor, none of this has been proven," said Drake.

"Bruce Lewis, CSC's chief counsel," said Sidney, "was indicted on drug trafficking charges yesterday."

"Is that correct, Mr. Drake?" asked the Judge, eyebrows gathering.

Drake stood up. "He's been arrested, but he hasn't been tried."

Sidney pressed on. "The CFO for CSC, who was also arrested on drug charges, was murdered in his jail cell just four months ago."

"Allegedly," said Drake.

"Your Chief Financial Officer did not hang himself from a bed sheet in his jail cell."

"He was a diagnosed manic depressive," said Drake. "We don't know what he did or didn't do."

"Oh, so he just happened to kill himself while we were searching for your financial records?" Sidney muttered, "Some coincidence."

"That's way there're called coincidences." Drake turned to the Judge. "It's our position that he killed himself."

"I guess the Police Chief also killed himself," challenged Sidney. "Shot himself through the heart, did he?"

"What!" said the Judge.

"What?" asked Drake. "Your Honor—"

"That's enough," said the Judge. Her clerk entered and slid a document onto the bench. The Judge glanced at the subject line—"Emergency Extradition Order." She said, "I have an urgent matter that requires my attention. We'll take a ten-minute recess." She banged her gavel, marched down the steps and out a side door.

As the door closed, Drake turned in his chair to huddle with a row of junior associates from his firm. His eyebrows were gathered. One client had been sentenced to death, shot and then disappeared. Another client had been indicted and arrested for drug trafficking on the spot. And the third client, the firm's biggest client, had nearly fired him. And that was just this week. He needed a win. After a minute passed, he felt a sharp fingernail poking him in the middle of his back. He turned his head. Drake had heard through the grapevine that Christina had been bitter since her last break-up. *What a waste,* he thought, as her perfume filled his thin nostrils. After whispering with his client, he approached Sidney. Seated, she was engaged in a deep conversation with a female staffer. The staffer wore a plain gray business suit, her long brunette hair pulled back in a simple silver clip.

Before he spoke, she asked, without looking up, "Where's your client?"

"She—"

"No, the other one," said Sidney, looking up. Her voice was low. The public didn't know that Alexander was missing yet, but she knew Drake had already been questioned by the FBI.

"I assume you mean Roger Alexander, because I hope you know where Bruce Lewis is, since you have him in custody."

"Assuming he hasn't escaped yet."

"I don't know where Roger Alexander is," said Drake, lowering his voice. "I have no interest in being charged for aiding and abetting a fugitive."

Sidney switched focus. "I believe Peter Savant was in the building the day the Attorney General was murdered. And I believe Christina Savant knows what happened." Sidney hadn't seen Peter Savant's face, but she was sure she had glimpsed him stepping into an elevator that day.

"You can't—"

"Not yet without a solid witness," said Sidney. "When we tested the purity of the heroin involved in all of this, this investigation went from a street-level heroin investigation to a multinational operation. Your client is in the middle of a very sophisticated drug distribution ring." Sidney leaned forward. "And people are dying."

"What purpose will these charges serve?" asked Drake. "It's a corporation. Peter Savant and our CFO are dead."

Sidney stood. "If you thought this was a waste of time, you wouldn't be standing over here."

"This is a complete waste of time. There's no purpose—"

"I can think of six purposes off the top of my head," said Sidney. "First, it'll probably shut you guys down." Sidney knew that Christina Savant was desperate to stop the hemorrhaging of her new company. "Second, if not, you'll have to forfeiture your ill-gotten gains. That should slow you down. Third, if the Savants try this again, it should drag them down. Fourth, it'll deter other legitimate companies. Fifth, it'll punish her company for putting the public at risk. Remember the folks with their 401(k) funds? Your stockholders who got screwed? And lastly, it'll put a smile on my face."

"You're going to hold the whole company responsible for the actions of a few?"

"Respondent superior," said Sidney. "I'm sorry, but the company is responsible for what its CEO and CFO does. These were not some junior employees."

"We don't know that they did any of this."

"Nathaniel, don't tell me that. They did it to me."

After ten minutes, Judge Lombard was again seated behind her bench. She gazed at Christina Savant. "First, you have my sincerest condolences on the death of your brother, particularly since he died in my courtroom. Hopefully, the conviction of his murderer has brought some solace to your family." She cleared her throat. "Because, this hearing will not."

Sidney turned and grinned at two of her friends seated in the courtroom.

Drake jumped to his feet. "Your Honor, Ms. Cox has not even considered other punishments. A substantial fine. Mandatory restitution. Or even judicial oversight for the company."

"Mr. Drake," said the Judge,` "You want to throw money at this? That's your solution?" Please have a seat."

He sat down.

"A grand jury will decide whether to charge Ms. Savant's company with criminal racketeering," said the judge. "A grand jury will be convened this Monday at nine in the morning. Court will now be adjourned." She banged her gavel.

THE SLIPPERY SLOPE
TO
HELL

CHAPTER 5

Thursday evening. Riding in a powerful sports car, Sidney and her childhood friend howled with laughter and beat their palms against the dashboard. They sang in unison, "We won, we won, we won."

From the backseat, "Hey, could someone up there, anyone up there, put a hand on the steering wheel?"

Sidney glanced out the window as they rapidly passed joggers, bikers, restaurants and short apartment buildings. Receding behind them were bead shops, coffee shops, and book shops.

"Oh, yeah," said Damian, the driver, "no problem, man, forgot about that." He grabbed the wheel, whipped onto "Q" Street and zipped the ice blue Lamborghini into a parallel parking space. He parked in front of a red brick building on a lovely tree-lined street.

Sidney turned to him and they grinned gleefully. In unison, they put their hands up, tickling their fingertips together like little kids.

In the backseat, Sidney's boyfriend smiled and rolled his eyes. "Does anyone care that I'm getting squashed back here in this two-door car from hell?"

"Missing your Lexus, Michael?" laughed Sidney. His four-door olive Lexus, parked nearby, did have decent leg room.

"Well . . . this is a very nice car, but next time, can we take the black Maserati? I'm sure that would be less packed." His words were tinged with playful sarcasm.

Dimples flexing, Sidney grinned over her shoulder. The custom-built car was all rich black leather, silver controls and dense carpeting, but Michael Hollander's knees were stuck in his chest. And they had made several stops along the way, including one so that she could change into black slacks.

Damian flicked a switch and the doors unlocked and swung upward. He glanced at Sidney seated in the passenger's seat. "After you, Counselor."

"No, after you, consultant to the greatest Task Force on planet Earth."

"I couldn't possibly," said Damian.

"Neither could—"

"Hello, catching a cramp back here."

They all stumbled out of the car, with Sidney pulling Michael out of the low-slung car. They stepped into the coolness of the evening. She heard metal jingle as she exhaled. All was right with her world. She absorbed the energy of Dupont Circle and smiled. The three of them danced and sang their way to Damian's front door.

As they stepped into the foyer of the three-level apartment, they were greeted with aromatic spices. Silver gourmet serving dishes adorned the table. Latin jazz played softly; a delicate shading of flute and percussion. A fire crackled in the fireplace. Warm shadows flickered over floral tapestries, gold-leaf framed pictures and crème-colored walls. The apartment was warm and elegant.

A young woman materialized from the kitchen. Sidney noticed that she had changed out of her plain gray business suit into a simple, long-sleeve black dress that hugged her slim figure. Short and athletic, her long brownish-black hair was still in a simple silver clip. Her bright eyes barely reflected her long work hours and even longer business trips. A white apron was tied around her waist and she held out a tray with four glasses of chilled champagne. While the others were taking their flutes, she dropped a light kiss on Damian's lips. Sidney looked from her gritty law school buddy to her coy best friend. While Damian did have a bronzed Italian complexion, a long black ponytail and an insolent grin, he was not "commitment man." As Sidney raised an eyebrow at Michael, she wondered about the last brunette who had popped out of the kitchen.

"Congratulations to us," Danielle said, setting the tray down and lifting her glass.

"There's still the hearing on Monday," said Michael.

Sidney smirked at him. He was a handsome, dark-skinned man with sharp brown eyes that were now scanning her face. His hair and mustache were freshly trimmed and he wore a beige suit and tie. Behind him, the television, turned to the evening news, was on mute.

"But we have every reason to be cautiously optimistic," he said.

Sidney hugged him. A criminal defense attorney with high-profile clients, he had proven to be a wonderful lawyer in her hour of need. And he had proven to be a great friend and a passionate lover since then.

"You're such a killjoy," said Damian, sipping his champagne.

Sidney released Michael. "I'm going to have to agree with Damian. The last two days have been—" She stopped as she glimpsed a mug shot of Roger Alexander on the muted television.

Damian picked up the remote and turned up the volume.

The anchor flicked her champagne blond locks and batted her sapphire eyes. "Tonight, we're bringing you an exclusive interview," she said, "from Wendy Shannon, the U.S. Attorney for the District of Columbia. You may recall that she recently won a highly publicized death verdict against the former Deputy Attorney General." The reporter whirled to face Wendy Shannon. Both women appeared grimly determined.

Sidney recognized the anchor. She had covered a political scandal in New York. For her efforts, she had been promoted to a national network. Sidney stepped toward the set as the reporter asked, "Who should we blame for the murder of Roger Alexander?"

"I'm not here to discuss that," said Shannon, straightening the lapels of a gray suit jacket.

"Is it the FBI's fault?" The reporter pulled out several newspapers. The page-one photo was of Charles Thomas in the middle of mayhem, looking skyward and flapping his arms in frustration. She had aired the same clip non-stop on her broadcast. "All of these papers are calling for the resignations of the FBI Director and his Deputy Director. In your opinion, should both men resign? The Director and Charles Thomas?"

"No, Charles . . . both men have done an outstanding job," said Shannon. "In fact, they—"

"But it's not your call whether they keep their jobs or not, is it?"

"That's really not the point. I—"

"A convicted felon was murdered while in their custody—"

"They were both appointed by President Wright," said Shannon. "And it's his decision to make."

"The rumor is that a big story is breaking. That the New York Times has a major scoop. A front-page story quoting senior administration officials as saying—"

"Anyone can write anything, but that doesn't make it—"

"It's written by a prize-winning journalist who broke a big scandal last year and—"

"And—"

"And, according to him, Roger Alexander is still alive." The reporter leaned forward. "That he either escaped or was kidnapped. Is that true?"

Shannon hesitated. "We don't know."

Caught off-guard by the major scoop, the reporter blinked rapidly. She opened her mouth and then shut it.

"I have someone here with me," said Shannon. "I'd like her to make an appeal."

A woman, in her seventies with a wide face and brilliant eyes, sat in the chair next to Wendy. She wore a loose-fitting, red ginger dress. "What do you want?" asked the older woman. A spitfire, she was crusty and hardcore.

"Just tell them what we discussed," directed Shannon.

The older woman faced the camera. Her jowls sagged and deep

lines creased her forehead. "I want to make an appeal to my boy," she said. "I've had a very long talk with the U.S. Attorney here and I am afraid for your safety. She wants you to turn yourself in." The woman faltered. "I . . . I—"

"It's okay," said Shannon, encouragingly.

"But I think you should—run!" Pumping her arms, she pointed vigorously at the camera. "What do you have to lose? You've already been convicted. I say—run!"

An hour later, Wendy Shannon sat in her temporary office at the Department of Justice. A special floor in the department had been set aside for the FBI-DEA Task Force. Only a small desk lamp lit the dark office. Out the window, behind her, the Washington Monument glowed in the soft moonlight. Her pine desk and navy couch were layered with criminal law treatises and brown manila folders.

Seated at her desk, Shannon crossed her arms and lay her forehead down on the stack of books and folders. Her short blonde hair fell forward. Her elbow was pressing against something hard. Without looking, she slid a cactus to the edge of the desk and dropped her new satellite cell phone into her pocket. She closed her eyes. How was it possible to make mistake after mistake? Every single time she got within a hair's breath of fixing her career, she screwed it up. First, it was the Lolita Valdez case. How could she have missed that memo? Then, it was the Sidney Cox case. She had been so sure of Sidney's guilt. If it had been left up to her, both Damian and Sidney would be sitting on death row right now. Now, after one of the biggest victories of her career, she had ruined it with this grand-standing fiasco. She had talked to that woman for an hour. Mrs. Alexander had given her no reason to believe she would turn on her. It had come right out of the bright blue sky. If you couldn't trust a seventy-eight year old woman, who could you trust?

Shannon groaned. Where had she gone wrong? She rolled her face to one side. It was the Valdez case. There was no way around that fact. That damn case was at the top of this twisted path she called a career. A garden-variety murder case, she had assigned it to an associate U.S. Attorney. He had charged Lolita Valdez with capital murder. However, as soon as Shannon learned that the murder was tied to a major FBI drug sting, she had wrestled the case away from him. A financial narcotics network was dismantled; eighty money launderers were arrested and sixty million in cash was discovered in airplanes, washing machines, refrigerators, and even toasters. At the time, she had thought it was the trial of the century, but she hadn't foreseen that the Attorney General would be killed in his own office.

Judge Lombard had presided over the Valdez case. The Puerto Rican Legal Defense Fund represented Valdez. New to the post and swamped, Shannon missed an FBI memo in the case file. A single page among thousands of pages. According to the memo, a key witness was wavering on his story. The FBI Director was on the stand when the bomb exploded. The defense counsel accused her and the Director of withholding exculpatory evidence. A breach of the law. A breach of ethics. A breach of common sense.

Judge Lombard declared a mistrial. Lolita Valdez was released from custody. However, not before she had been brutalized. She was later locked up in St. Elizabeth's Mental Hospital.

The press was all over the story. Under fire, Shannon had pointed the finger at the FBI Director. Unfortunately for her, he had produced the FBI memo. Fortunately for her, it had been sent to the associate attorney. Shannon tossed her file copy of the memo into the trash and publicly fired the assistant for incompetence. Shannon had barely clung to her job. The Attorney General was furious. The FBI Director was furious. Judge Lombard was furious. But, most importantly, the President of the United States of America was furious. Now, Lolita Valdez was dead.

No one knew how sorry she was by what happened; nevertheless, here she was all over again. Filled with hurt and regret,

Shannon heard a soft knock at the door and raised her head. "Come in," she said softly.

The door opened slowly. Charles Thomas was standing there. A dim hall light illuminated him in the doorway. Their eyes locked. Neither spoke.

"Are you angry?" asked Shannon.

"You're like the duchess of doom." His voice was gentle.

She exhaled, a half smile on her lips. "If you can't be nice, at least have the courtesy to be vague."

He didn't move. His hand stayed on the doorknob. "What were you thinking?"

"I don't know what to say."

"That's what you always say."

She chewed the inside of her lip and waited.

He leaned against the door jamb. "We've been working on this investigation night and day for a year and a half, and you go and do this." He studied her. "You scare me. You're impulsive. You're unpredictable."

"Isn't that what you love about me?" said Shannon.

Silence.

She pushed her chair back and rose slowly from her desk. As she crossed the room, she reached for the top button of her gray suit jacket. She unbuttoned it. She watched his brown eyes move to the top button. She unbuttoned the second button.

"I don't want this, Wendy," said Thomas. "Not anymore."

Her fingers worked down the rest of her jacket buttons. Underneath, she was wearing a see-through black camisole. She watched his eyes move across her breasts. "Are you sure?" She stopped in the middle of the room. She slipped the jacket down her arms. "You're positive?" She dropped the jacket to the floor. His dark eyes followed the jacket and then went back up to her. He watched her every movement.

"I'm not some boy-toy."

"What does that have to do with anything?" Her hands disappeared behind her back. The only sound in the room was a slow unzipping. Her black skirt fell to the floor. She stepped out of it and kicked it to the side. She wore a black garter belt and sheer black stockings. "You have a decision to make, cupcake," she said.

"What's that?"

"Come in and get ready," she said, strolling to him, "or shut the door and go home."

With one hand, he reached out and pulled her against his chest. With the other hand, he slammed the door shut.

———

Later, after Sidney and Michael left his home, Damian stripped and stepped down into his Jacuzzi. Black porcelain, it was sleek and luxurious. Settling into a sculpted seat, he sank into the warmth of the bubbly water. He flipped a switch on an electronic control panel and steamy water jetted out, massaging his toned muscles. The dark hair on his muscular forearms was slick against his olive skin. The lights were dim and vanilla-scented French candles dotted the black tiles surrounding the Jacuzzi. Soft music flowed. Damian closed his eyes. He breathed in deeply. He slowly realized that he had flipped the switch. A smile crossed his lips. He was finally on the right side of the law. He had finally made things right with Sidney. He was finally waiting on a woman of substance.

Still, Damian allowed time to fade away as he returned to the night when his life had come to a fork in the road. It was like any other Saturday night. Neither he nor Sidney had a high school date. After crawling in bumper-to-bumper traffic on the narrow tree-lined streets near the Tidal Basin, Damian had parked his aunt's car near Haines Point. They had perched on the enormous bronze sculpture of a man emerging from the ground. In the distance, a full moon had illuminated the rounded marble crest of the Jefferson Memorial. Neither of them had been prepared for their lives to change forever.

"A glass of wine for your thoughts?"

He opened his eyes as Danielle entered the room. She was

nude and she carried two glasses of white wine. She stepped down into the warm water and handed one to Damian.

"Thank you," said Damian. He took a sip. He felt the alcohol relax his muscles. "Dinner was wonderful. What did you call the main course?"

"A seafood stew call moqueca."

"Moqueca?" he asked. "Is it Colombian?"

"Unfortunately, my ancestors can't claim it. It's actually an African dish from Bahia, Brazil." She sipped her wine. "When the Africans arrived in Brazil, they brought their own cooking skills, mixing hot spices in with Portuguese and Indian dishes. It's amazing what can be done with a little palm oil, coconut milk, onions, tomatoes—"

"Some lobster and a delicious cook," said Damian without blinking. He didn't realize it, but his long eyelashes were damp, making him look sexy as hell.

She smiled as she sipped her wine.

He watched her lips touch the rim of the glass. Her pink tongue darted out, flicking a drop of wine from the rim. He set his glass down on the black tile behind him. Moving toward her, he took her glass and set it down. Settling back in his seat, he reached out, took her small hand and pulled her to him. His hand slid behind her head and unsnapped the silver clip holding her hair. His damp hands fanned her hair around her face. Her long hair floated in the water and against her slender shoulders. Her hand slid behind his head and slipped a rubber band off his dark ponytail. She fanned his hair around his face. She then leaned into him, kissing his forehead and the end of his nose.

"I could just scoop you up with a spoon," said Damian, pulling her between his wet thighs.

———

As they drove from Dupont Circle, comfortably seated in his olive Lexus, Sidney ran her hand up Michael's thigh.

"All right, girl," he said, clearing his throat, "don't start something you can't finish."

Her hand moved further up his thigh.

The car swerved. "Watch yourself now," he said.

"You just watch the road," said Sidney, moving her hand up. He blinked slowly and inhaled.

Sidney's eyes shifted from him to the speedometer, which ticked upward. She glanced out as they passed an aging RFK Stadium. Tall street lights cast a dim yellow glow over Southeast Washington. They were heading out of the District toward Prince George's County. On their way to Michael's house, they would pass by the new Maryland stadium. She and her father had yet to make any of the Redskin's games out there, but hope sprang eternal.

By the time they turned off Center Street into Mitchellville, a new community with luxury homes, Michael was in a low pant. Gripping the steering wheel, he turned left and then right and then into the driveway of his two-story tan brick home. Sidney laughed to herself as she watched Michael drive more like Damian than himself. He cut the ignition, turned, gently grasped Sidney's upper arms, pressed her against the seat and kissed her deeply. His cologne filled her senses. Her breathing deepened.

"You drive me crazy," said Michael, releasing her.

"I'm just getting started," said Sidney. "Get out of the car."

Throwing the car door open, Michael shot out of the car. As he slammed the door shut, he glimpsed the keys still in the ignition. He opened the car door, grabbed the keys, shut the door, and circled to the passenger side. He was there before Sidney opened her door. So he opened her door with flourish and helped her from the car. They both laughed.

"Come here, woman," he said. Kissing her, he pressed her against the car. He pulled away and glanced around his neighborhood. "Let's take this into the house," he said. His voice was husky.

"Are you sure?" teased Sidney.

"Oh, yeah."

They ran across the front lawn. Sidney grinned as he tried to appear cool, but dropped his keys before he finally got the front door open. As they stumbled through the door, they were fumbling with buttons, jackets, a blouse, a shirt, slacks, and a pair of pants. They were pushing clothes up, down and off.

Lying on his back on her navy office couch, Charles Thomas opened his eyes. He gazed up at Wendy. Her hands and body were moving. He said softly, "Stop."

Ignoring him, her hands and body continued to move.

"I'm serious." He reached up and held her forearms. "I've met someone else."

Shannon stopped and stared down into his eyes. "What?"

"I'm sick of this. I don't know what this is. This is some weird, secret office fling thing, but it's been going on for months now."

"Well, you said—"

"Forget what I said. This is killing me," he said.

She blinked twice.

"You can't love me," he said, "because you don't even like yourself. You don't have any hobbies, no cat, no dog, no fish. Just a dead cactus."

Shannon sat up, tucking a strand of blonde hair behind her ear. "That was an office gift."

"That was an office joke," he said. "Never mind the obvious differences here—we have different ethics, principles, friends. In that, I actually have some."

Silence.

"If you had some," said Shannon, "you'd have told me about the Task Force meetings," she said. "But I have to hear about it. It's humiliating."

"Is that what all this hostility has been about? Some meetings?" He leaned his head to one side. "Wendy, if you didn't act the way you do, you'd get invited to the big meetings. But nobody ever knows what you're going to do." He watched her recline against the back of the couch. She looked resigned. "I saw you on television tonight and I still have no idea what you were doing. It's just like the Valdez case. You make these crazy mistakes and then you're too embarrassed to own up to them. You blame somebody else and then you go after them with guns loaded." He frowned. "That's wrong. Do you have any morals at all?"

"Said the naked man," said Shannon.

"Touché," chuckled Thomas. "But still—"

Silence.

"You think you know me," she said, shifting to stand up.

Sitting up, he grabbed her hand and pulled her into his lap. "You think I don't know you." He gazed into her gray eyes. "That I haven't taken my time to get to know you? You're always terrified. You're terrified somebody's going to figure out you're not good enough for this job. You're terrified your father won't ever approve of you. Which is why you wear the same eyeglasses he wears." He glanced at the round-rimmed glasses on her desk. "You're terrified that you finally have everything you've always wanted. That your career is on the rise. That you're in charge of one of the biggest cases in the country. That you're the center of attention. That you're in the limelight," he said. "And you're terrified that you're going to fail."

She exhaled. "Then why do you want to be with me?"

"I have no freakin' idea," he said.

They laughed.

"You smoke," he said. "You drink. You lie in the sun with no hat and no sunscreen. You're clogging your arteries with beef and pork that's prepared so rare, I wonder why you bother to cook it at all."

"I quit smoking."

"Since when?" asked Thomas.

She glanced away, sheepishly. "Why should I bother? You don't believe anything I say anyway."

He wrapped his arms around her waist. "You're not saving anything for old age. I saw your driver's license. You're an organ donor? Are you trying to kill somebody?"

She giggled. "Is that all?"

"Well . . ."

"Well?" asked Shannon. "Well what?"

"Well . . . your housekeeping . . . how can I put this? You're a slob. All you need is a snout and a tail."

She laughed.

After a minute, she leaned against his warm chest. She rested quietly. She sat up. "So you're the clean-cut, straight-laced, mass-attending, long-distance-running vegetarian—with one flaw?"

He pointed at her as she pointed to herself.

Thomas said, "It took you all of fifteen minutes to ask me to bed. But you have yet to ask me to spend the night."

"So you're going to leave me for someone else?" asked Shannon.

"This is no way to live. Let me help you." He gazed into her gray eyes. "Let me love you or let me go."

———————————

Danielle gazed into the dark eyes of her lover. She eased back, moving easily through the water of the Jacuzzi. She asked in a soft voice, "Damian, can we talk?"

Lost in a comfort haze, Damian blinked. "Huh?"

"Can we talk?"

"We are talking."

"You know what I mean."

"We've had a lovely evening. Is this going to be a turn of events?" smiled Damian.

"It depends on your perspective," said Danielle.

"Alrighty then," said Damian, sitting up. "Let's have at it."

"We've been going out for months now," said Danielle. "Is this a serious thing?"

"I thought that you, Ms. Law and Order, were having difficulty getting involved with a former drug dealer?"

"You said you were reformed. Were you mistaken?"

Damian moved to stand up, getting out of the water. "You don't know me at all," he said.

She held his damp forearm and drew him back into the water.

She moved close to him, nuzzling his damp chest. She ran her hand through the hairs on his chest. "I know who you are," she said, locking eyes with him. "I know that you go out with lots of women. That you treat them all very well—fancy dinners, expensive trips, beautiful flowers." She had heard all about Damian's exploits during a law school vacation with Sidney. "I also know that you back away when things get serious."

He turned his head.

Holding his chin gently, she turned his head to face her. "I know you're hurt by your parents' rejection. I know they walked away after you and Sidney were arrested in high school. I understand you're working hard to try to right the wrongs you committed. I understand why you had to choose the lifestyle you had after spending years in prison. I understand what it means to you to be working at the Department of Justice." She gazed at him. "You haven't said so, but I understand your need to show the world that you are an honorable man," she said. "But I don't need that. I don't need any of that. I understand who and what you are."

"I can't give—" said Damian.

"I won't always be here for you, Damian."

"Are you giving me an—"

"Let me be there for you," said Danielle. "Let me be your wife."

———————

Lying on a soft beige couch in his home, Michael Hollander pulled the ivory comforter around Sidney. For his efforts, she snuggled closer to him. He felt the warmth of her lean back against his chest and stomach. He kissed the back of her head and his arm tightened around her narrow waist. From the pale moon light that flowed into the house, he could see a headless Barbie doll tossed into a corner. After a few minutes, he raised himself on one elbow. He watched her closely. "Sidney, there's something I need to tell you," he said. He felt her body stiffen in his arms.

"Nothing good ever follows that sentence," said Sidney.

"My ex-wife is moving back to D.C. with our two kids."

"What? Where have I been?" She turned to look up at him. Silence.

"I thought you said she had met some clown up in New York," said Sidney.

"I'm guessing that didn't work out," he said.

"I don't understand—"

"Sidney, we've spent nearly every day together since what, June or July, and I've gotten to know you pretty well."

"What does that have to do with—"

"You make list of everything—on anything. You're an information junkie. *CNN*, *Headline News*, *Washington Post*, *Newsweek*, *Essence*, *People* and *Soap Opera Digest*." He saw her smile. "Yeah, I saw it and I know you read it. Your best day is a balmy eighty degrees with a light breeze . . . and you're outdoors." He paused. "You're always cold." He pulled the comforter more tightly around her. "You're an excellent driver, but you don't know jack about cars. You can do an Aerobics III Class, but you can't run down the block. Your favorite dish is steamed scallops and rice pilaf. Your favorite dessert is pecan pie. Little things irritate you, like misplacing your stapler, but you didn't bat an eye when you crashed your new Celica. Your world isn't right if you don't talk to your best girlfriend in New York every Sunday, and Damian on Saturdays, and although you squabble with your parents, particularly with your mother, you were petrified when they almost split up."

Silence.

He could feel her breath on his cheek. "And that you look like Kizzy when you wake up in the morning," he said, smiling.

They both laughed.

"I do not," said Sidney. "Do I?"

He looked down at her. "You're exquisite."

Silence.

"Tell me, what this has to do with your ex-wife?" said Sidney.

"I also know that you haven't even looked for an apartment here. You're living at your parents' house. You're renting a car.

There's no artwork or pictures up in your office. All your stuff is still in storage in New York."

"You think I'm not staying?"

"You're living a temporary existence," said Michael. "Nothing about you is permanent."

"But my car was totaled," said Sidney.

"That was months ago."

"I don't know what you want me to say," said Sidney.

"I want you to say that you're over your two-year relationship with William Fitzgerald. I want you to say that the reason he's been hanging around and calling you all hours of the day and night has to do with something financial. That even though he's been laid off by Salomon Brothers, that all he wants is your money—and not you."

"He hurt me, Michael."

"I know that. I hate it that he hurt you. I know he wasn't there for you when everything went wrong . . . but I was." He gazed into her eyes. "I know what it's like to be hurt. I was hurt and angry when my marriage failed. I really loved Vanessa. And she didn't ask for much, just my time." He hesitated. "Maybe I used that to control the relationship. I don't know . . ." He looked away. "But I don't want to get in too deep here . . . if this is a dead-end relationship."

"I—"

"Did you just move down here to shake William up?" asked Michael.

"That's not fair," said Sidney.

"Maybe not, but it's real."

"You've had more time to get over your marriage—"

"I know you thought your future was with him. In New York. But now, it's time to think about a new life. Here . . . with me."

Thirty seconds later. "Eh?" asked Wendy Shannon. "Love?" She stared at Charles Thomas in her office at the Justice Department.

"I think I just went deaf." A phone rang. Shannon looked toward a pile of clothes on the floor. She slid off his lap.

"How's that deaf theory holding up?" said Thomas, watching her from the couch.

She hesitated and then searched the floor for her suit jacket. Clothes were everywhere. Her gray jacket was underneath his black slacks and her camisole. Kneeling, she found the cell phone in the pocket, answered the call, listened, stood up and then hung up. She darted around the office, gathering her clothes.

"Going somewhere?" He stretched his arms along the back of the couch.

"I've got . . . a . . . an emergency . . . yep, that's it . . . I need to go."

A red light from her cell phone flashed in the darkness.

"How come you never recharge that thing?" he asked calmly. "One day, you're really going to need it."

She was balancing on one foot, pulling on sheer stockings. "I'm sure you're right. You're always right." She slipped a red security badge around her neck.

"Are you running out on me?"

Now that she was fully dressed again, she backed toward the door. "Don't be silly." She bolted out the door. She leaned against the wall in the hallway. "Oh, no."

Thirty seconds later. "Huh?" asked Damian Stagel. "Wife?" He stared at Danielle Sanchez in his apartment in Dupont Circle. A phone rang.

"Don't answer that," said Danielle.

Damian jumped out of the Jacuzzi, answered his ringing cell phone, dried off, got dressed and headed for the door. He cut through warm wonderful scents—stew and burning kindling—lingering in the air. At the front door, he turned and shouted, "I'll . . . I'll be right back." He stepped out of the front door and shut it. He leaned against the front door. "Oh, man."

Thirty seconds later. "What?" asked Sidney Cox. "New life?" She stared at Michael Hollander in his Mitchellville home. A phone rang.

"Sidney, come on—" he started as she answered her phone and then listened.

Sidney clicked off her cell phone, leapt off the couch, got dressed, headed for the door, turned and said, "There's a . . . a . . . problem at the office, I got to go." She shut the front door and leaned against it. "Ah, shit."

THE GREAT GET-AWAY

CHAPTER 6

Thursday night. Wendy Shannon stepped out of the elevator into the lobby of the Justice Department. Moving quickly, the elaborate mosaic walls became a blur. A red security badge swung from her neck chain as she passed the night guard without a word. She ignored the way he scrunched up his face as she passed. She stepped out of the glass double doors and into the coolness of late October.

Deep in thought, she circled the building to a dark, nearly empty parking lot. Being in a relationship was like voluntarily committing yourself to an insane asylum. Breathing in deeply, Shannon patted her pockets. Where were her cigarettes? She needed a serious nicotine fix. No cigarettes, just a phone. She realized with a jolt that she had turned into her mother. Somewhere along the line between birth and forty-two, she had morphed into her mother. Her father had not known it, but his wife had been a chain smoker. She frequently smoked in the bathroom. The telltale sign was a good dose of tropical air freshener. As a child, Shannon had been curious about these bathroom sabbaticals. From time to time, she had pressed her ear to the door. She had heard crying, quiet and frustrated. When her mother emerged, her smile was fixed in place. Had her mother lived a life of quiet desperation? Providing every creature comfort to his small family, her father, a silver-haired and distinguished judge, had been emotionally distant. With little thought, Shannon had patterned herself after him. She had become cold and distant, disregarding her own mother. Shannon stopped in the middle of the parking lot. Her mother had been disregarded. She had juggled work, kids, a household, and two matching sets of aging grandparents. And she had been disregarded.

Shannon looked around and spotted her metallic green car among the few cars in the lot. Unlocking the car door, she got in, put the key in the ignition, and slammed the door shut. She took a deep breath. *Gotta have a cigarette*, she thought. She rifled through her purse. Nothing. She frowned. She opened her console. She scowled. She slammed it shut. She turned, peering into the backseat. She pursed her lips. She bent over and looked under the front seats. She sat up. She pulled down the visor. She pulled down the other visor. She lay over the car seats and tugged at the glove compartment. It was locked. The lengths she went to protect herself from herself. Exhaling, she pulled a key out of her purse and unlocked the glove compartment. Relief flowed through her. She pulled out three cartons of cigarettes. The dark silence of the car was filled with the crinkling of clear plastic. With the carton open and without sitting up, she picked out a slim cigarette, flicked her lighter, slid the cigarette between her lips and dragged on it. The scent of lit tobacco filled the car. White swirls spun in the black air.

As she relaxed against the seats, the car door whipped open. Cool air rushed into the car. Someone grabbed her feet. Her face hit the passenger seat. *Charles could not be this mad*, she thought. She turned her head as she was being yanked out of the car. She didn't recognize the face. She glanced around. Men surrounded the car. She kicked and made contact with a pointy heel. A man yelled. She yelled. He stopped yelling and resumed yanking. She kept yelling and resumed kicking. Her feet were grabbed again. Now, there were more hands, strong hands around her ankle. She was being pulled out of the car. She heard the other car doors unlock. Someone must have hit the automatic button. She glimpsed the other car doors opening.

She grabbed the steering wheel. They pulled harder. She clung harder. They pulled harder. She hung on. A man entered from the passenger side and peeled her hands from the steering wheel. She opened her mouth and sank her teeth into the skin of his hand. He shrieked and drew back. She grabbed the wheel again. Another man reached in and slammed his fist into her hands. "Awww!" she screamed. She released the steering wheel, but grabbed her lit cigarette on the way out. Her face and hands banged against the car seat and dashboard as she was dragged to the pavement. It was cold and hard, and smelled of gasoline. The wind was knocked out of her. Gasping for air, she kicked one assailant and burned another on the hand with her cigarette. As a multitude of hands reached for her, she burned as many of them as she could. They backed away with screeches as she scrambled back into the car and slammed her door.

She quickly turned the key in the ignition. Black sedans appeared out of nowhere. She slammed on the accelerator. She rammed a car. Her body was thrown forward into the steering wheel. Her chest felt bruised. A hand entered the open passenger door. She reached across the passenger seat and slammed the door shut. She heard a loud squeal. She had slammed the hand in the car door. "Take that," she shouted. She threw the car in reverse and hit the accelerator. She rammed into a car behind her. Her gray eyes flew to the rearview mirror. Cars were on all sides. With a sneer, a man stepped in front of her car. She narrowed her eyes and hit the accelerator. He leapt to the left, but not before she ran over his right foot. She glanced around in desperation. The lot was empty. How many times had Charles warned her about this lot? She was trapped. She honked her horn. Maybe Charles would hear her. *Even if he did, how far would he go to save her?* she wondered.

As the men moved toward the car, she unlocked the door, jumped out, and scrambled up on the hood of one of the black sedans and screamed at the top of her lungs. "Charles!" A hand reached for her ankle. She looked down and saw a reddish-pink cigarette burn. She stomped on it. Now he was screaming and she was screaming. "Charles!" she cried again. As she turned, she felt someone jam a syringe in her butt.

In Dupont Circle, Damian Stagel strode down the walkway of his small front yard. He wore stingray-skin cowboy boots and a Yankees' baseball cap. Around him, three-bay row houses spiraled out from Connecticut, Massachusetts and New Hampshire Avenues. He thought about Danielle. She definitely had his number. His mother had told me once that the first sign of insanity was repeating the same thing over and over again and expecting a different result. He was not any good at relationships. If he was, wouldn't he be on speaking terms with his own parents? After all, these were the very people who had brought him here. Weren't they at least obligated to care? He thought about the long-legged brunette from the summer. She had looked great, even in the morning. A smile crossed his lips. What was her name? Had he lost her phone number? If so, he could probably find her apartment. Wasn't it right around here, somewhere? Danielle crossed his mind. She would bust his balls if he strayed. The smile faded from his lips. What to do?

When Damian reached his car, his dark eyes swept over the street. Why were there so many cars parked in Dupont Circle on a Thursday night? His brow furrowed. When he returned, he would park the ice blue sports car in a nearby garage with his other cars. Unlocking it, he slid behind the wheel, dropped his cell phone in the passenger seat, and turned the key in the ignition. Nothing. His eyebrows knitted. He tried again. A click and a purr. He glimpsed something silver on the floor. He leaned across the car seats. He picked up Sidney's car keys and her tiny silver mace canister. He rose and did a double-take at the pistol pointed at his car window.

Seconds ticked by. The man motioned with a finger. Damian flicked a switch and the window slid down.

"Get out."

Damian didn't move.

Frowning, the man opened his mouth. Damian whipped out the can of mace and sprayed him in the eyes and mouth. The man screamed, grabbed his eyes and staggered backwards. Damian glanced around. He didn't see anyone else. He shoved his door open, slamming the man in the face. Damian heard a crack as the door connected with the man's head. The man fell to the ground. Damian stepped out of the car and looked down at the man. The caustic odor of the mace hung in the air. With narrowed eyes, Damian glanced around again and noticed black sedans. FBI? Drug dealers from his former life? He glanced back at the man on the ground. Standing near his midsection, Damian swung his booted foot backwards and then stopped mid-swing. From the corner of his eye, he spotted men sprinting toward him. He turned. He saw at least three guns in three different hands. He glanced back at his front door. Could he make it back inside? Had he double-bolted the door? None of the men were headed that way. Damian took off on foot in the other direction. Had he set the security system? Was Danielle still in the Jacuzzi? Running hard, he patted his pockets. A wallet, but no cell phone.

In the darkness, Damian turned and ran down "Q" Street. He passed boutiques, coffee shops and hair salons as he raced down the street. He turned left and ran through a 24-hour book store. His eyes darted around the book store. He did not recognize anyone. He ran out the back and through the back restaurant area. Could he beat them back to his apartment? He heard the men behind him. He ran around the tables. Patrons watched him in shock. He dashed out onto the sidewalk, bumping into thick crowds of people. Instead of leading them back to his place, he darted down 19th Street, passing a green Starbuck's. The sweet smell of cinnamon wafted by him. Underneath his shirt, sweat trickled down the black hair on his chest and down his firm abdomen. His long legs pumped as he raced down his street, dodging cars coming head on. He glanced over his shoulder. The men were still coming after him.

Damian looked ahead. A white classical fountain stood in the middle of Dupont Circle Park, encircled by two long rows of black benches. Great elms met overhead, shading the men sitting, talking, and drinking in the park. Thick lines of traffic circled the park. Cars were heading off in all directions. Some stopped at the various street lights circling the park; other drivers were either lost or oblivious to the stop lights. Damian caught his breath and headed into the traffic. He was nearly struck by a blue Audi. He leapt over the car hood and then darted around a yellow Mustang. The Mustang screeched to a halt. Without turning, he heard the squeal of tires and the crumpling of metal. He glanced over his shoulder and ran into a motorcycle. They both went down. His knees and elbows banged into the pavement and a hard rubber tire. His baseball cap flew off. Catching his breath, he pulled the stunned rider to her feet. Gazing at him, her eyes softened.

"Sorry, I—" started Damian, as he glanced back. Without another word, he dashed through the park, leaping over a black bench. He darted around the men in the park. Some wore business suits; other wore jeans and tennis shoes. He crossed the park and took a left. He ran past three avenues, took several turns, his eyes searching for a pay phone, before he headed down a small narrow tree-lined street. He recognized a pale yellow, four-story apartment building with the small front yard. "Thank God," he whispered. Then he saw her standing under the dim yellow light cast by an old-fashioned lamp post. Relief flooded his body as he ran faster. Then panic set in. Jesus, what was her name? Name? Name? Name? Barbara? Betty? Beth? Was it Beth? He hoped to god it was.

"Beth!" he shouted, racing toward her. She turned with a radiant smile. She was brunette, long-legged, wearing a short elegant evening dress, matching handbag, and heels. Her make-up was flawless; her diamond earrings dazzling.

As Damian neared her, he saw her smile fade and then he saw a man exit the building behind her. The man's eyes followed her gaze and they both stared at Damian as he rushed toward them. Reaching them, Damian stopped abruptly, at a loss for words.

She looked on coyly. "Tom," she said, "this is Damian. Damian, this is my date."

Damian stuck out his hand. "Nice to meet you, man."

Confused, date-man looked from Beth to Damian and said, "Sure . . . nice to meet you, too."

"Great," said Damian. He grabbed Beth by the shoulders, spun her around and pushed her back into the building. Her date stared, perplexed. When he moved toward the double-glass doors, Damian slammed it shut.

"Can I come upstairs?" asked Damian. "Just for a moment?"

Beth whirled on him. "I met someone new. I won't take you back."

"I understand," said Damian. He pushed her toward the elevator.

"It took me months to get over you," she said. "Waiting for you to call."

When they reached the elevator, he pressed the button, watching the white light bounced from floor to floor. He glanced over his shoulder at the double doors. The men were in the process of tripping over her date. He looked down at Beth. She hadn't noticed. Her eyes were on him. The elevator doors popped open and he shoved her inside. He pressed the button for the second floor.

"I knew you'd be back," she said.

On the second floor, he grabbed her, pulling her out of the elevator and toward the middle of the long hall. "I need to use your phone."

"Who are you calling?" she asked, stopping in front of her apartment door and unlocking her door.

Rushing into her apartment ahead of her, Damian can feel the heat of her stare on his back. He dropped a key ring on an end table, grabbed her phone and started to dial.

She glanced down at the phone, recognized his number and frowned. "Who are you calling?"

"Danielle," he said.

She reached around him and hung up the phone. "Get out."

"You don't understand."

"Better than you think," she said.

"I've seen you with her in the same Starbucks where I met you. Does she have any idea that you're going to wine and dine her right up to the night you dump her?"

"Beth, I—" started Damian. He saw the hurt in her eyes. "I had no idea," he said.

She looked up at the sincere gleam in his dark eyes. She leaned her head to one side. She then haul back and slapped him. Hard. "Now you do."

His ears were ringing. He shook his head to clear his thoughts. "That's for revisiting the scene of the crime," she said.

They stared at each other. His eyes were confused. Hers were hurt and angry.

Damian put a hand to his stinging jaw. "I swear I'll fix this . . . somehow . . . but I just need to make one quick call," he said. He grabbed for the phone.

She grabbed for his key ring. She pointed the canister of mace at his face. "Get out."

Damian raised both hands. "Okay, okay," he said, backing out the door.

Standing in the hallway, staring into the canister of mace, Damian heard a ping. He glanced down the hall. The elevator doors slid open. Turning his head, he glanced to his left. There was a window at the other end of the hall. He glanced to his right. Three men rushed toward him. Dropping his hands, he raced toward the window. He yanked it up. It didn't budge. "No, no, no." He scanned it. It was locked. He unlocked it. He pulled it up again. The cool night air hit his face. He glanced down two floors at the grass below. He glanced back at the men. They were halfway to him. He threw both legs out the window, prayed and then let go. Cold air rushed past his ears. He slammed hard into the ground. It knocked the wind out of him. Lying on his back, he stared up at the men. They were debating whether to jump or not.

Damian jumped up, circled the building and raced down the street. He spotted a yellow taxi. He ran down the sidewalk, even with the cab, and when the cab stopped at a red light, he ran into the street in front of it. He waved both arms. The taxi stopped. He jumped into the back seat. He thumped into the biggest man he had ever seen in his life. The man was blonde, blue-eyed, dressed in a dark blue suit and was huge. His wife was the same. They conversed rapidly in what might have been Norwegian.

The hulk then turned to Damian and said, "Get out."

"Why does everybody keep saying that to me?" asked Damian.

Looking out the back window, Damian saw several men running toward the cab. He turned, planning to plead his case with Mr. and Mrs. Hulk. Unfortunately, he was staring down the barrel of a gun.

"Is everybody in this city armed?" asked Damian.

"Get out."

His fellow passengers shoved him out the door. The cab sped off as he hit the pavement. Damian looked up. Guns were pointed at his face.

———————

Minutes later, Sidney Cox closed the front door. As she crossed the front lawn, she fished her keys out of her purse. When she reached her red rental car, she glanced down at the keys. "Damn," she whispered. She had Michael's keys. She glanced back at his tan brick house and then at his car. He had said she could use it whenever she wanted. After quibbling with herself, she set her jaw, slipped into the olive Lexus, backed it out of the driveway, and drove away from the quiet neighborhood.

As she turned onto Center Street, a main thoroughfare in Mitchellville, Maryland, her thoughts drifted as she maneuvered the large car through the traffic. She had really been caught off guard by Michael. According to her limited experience, relationships were doom-in-a-can. Two years with a haughty unsupportive asshole—that would be William—and two years with a fun, sensuous, and talented reggae singer—that would be the penniless pauper—the one-who-shall-not-be-named—had been enough. She sighed.

However, setting the pauper aside, she thought, was Michael right about William? Had she moved down here to jerk his chain? He had disappointed her more than once. There was the time when she sprained her ankle and he was too busy with a securities transaction to check on her. And last year, when she had been nauseous with pneumonia, he had flown to Paris on business instead of taking her to the emergency room. Oh, yeah, and there was that time when she was locked up in a federal penitentiary, accused of murder.

Now that William was unemployed, and now that she was cleared, he seemed to have so much more time for her. Peach roses were arriving like clockwork. But maybe it wasn't about her. Maybe it was about the CSC stock planted in her safety deposit box by Roger Alexander. But, on the other hand, did she really own it? She hadn't paid for it. It wasn't a gift. After this was all over, she would look into it. Perhaps the real question was "How much time did she really want to spend pondering some guy's motives?" *Enough already,* she thought.

As she changed lanes, she wondered whether it was really them or her. Was she negligent in choosing her relationships? Or was she killing them off with malice aforethought? Sighing, she thought about Michael. He had seemed a bit annoyed as she made two quick phone calls, said good-bye, and then raced out the door.

Sidney stopped at a red light on Center Street. The four-lane highway was a straight shot back into the District. It was lined by strip malls and large warehouses. She checked her rearview mirror. How long had that dark sedan been behind her? She glanced at the other lanes. There were several black sedans behind her. Was it a coincidence? She glanced to her left. A black sedan. She glanced to her right. A black sedan. She looked at the driver. He met her eyes and raised an eyebrow. Turning, Sidney focused on the street light. When it turned green, she floored her accelerator. Who were they? The FBI had warned them about retaliation from drug dealers. She darted in and around several cars ahead of her. She glanced in her rearview mirror. The sedans gave chase.

Keeping her eyes on the road, her hand searched her purse. Where in the blue blazes was her cell phone? She rolled her eyes when she realized that she had left it on Michael's table. She leaned over, opening his glove compartment. It was neatly organized. There was no cell phone, but there was something better. She reached in and pulled out a .38 pistol. She closed the compartment and put the gun in her lap. Later, she would have to have a conversation with Michael about gun control. She looked up. A blue BMW was about a foot from her front bumper. She slammed on her brakes and then swerved into the left lane. She pressed the accelerator to the floor. The car shot forward. She preferred small cars, but was learning to appreciate the power of this one.

She glimpsed a green highway exit sign. She hit her brakes, dropped behind the blue car and grabbed the steering wheel, yanking it to the right. She cut off several black sedans. As she circled down the exit ramp, black sedans shot past the exit. However, two exited. She sped down the ramp and raced toward the District.

Within a few minutes, she was racing through stop signs on North Carolina Street, a dark and quiet tree-lined street. Luckily, the traffic was light on the narrow streets of the residential neighborhood. Orange Halloween pumpkins decorated front stoops. As she entered a large intersection, she glimpsed a church van. The driver was looking the other way. Sidney slammed on her brakes. Her car slid. With tires squealing, the large car stopped inches from the van. The driver turned, his mouth open. As the driver recovered and the van turned away, black sedans arrived from all directions. Doors were slamming everywhere. Blocked in by the sedans, men approached her car, brandishing weapons.

"Oh, my God," said Sidney. Adrenaline flowed through her body. One of them motioned for her to get out of the car. He pointed a .357 magnum. She gritted her teeth. She also gripped the gun lying across her lap as she opened the car door. She eased out of the car, standing behind the car door and holding the gun down at her side. One of the men, she assumed the leader, limped toward her.

"Who the hell are you?" asked Sidney.

"You're in no position to ask questions," he said.

Still standing behind the car door, she raised the gun and pointed it with both hands. She rested her arms on the top of the car door.

"Who the hell are you?" repeated Sidney.

"You don't have the nerve to shoot."

"Really?" asked Sidney. "You don't know the year I've had."

He stepped toward her. She fired. His eyes widened. He screamed, grabbing his head. Blood trickled through his fingers as he went down. Were those reddish-pink burns on the back of his hand? The other men leaped behind their cars. The man jumped up, holding his ear. He started toward Sidney. She cocked the gun. Angry, he continued to move. She pulled the trigger again. Click. She pulled the trigger again. Click. No bullets. "Why must there always be a problem?" asked Sidney. She scrambled back into the car, slammed the door and threw the car in reverse. She slammed on the accelerator. The car shot backwards, slamming into a sedan. She grinned when her big car demolished the smaller vehicle, dragging it backwards. She yanked the steering wheel to the right and drove up onto the sidewalk around the other sedans.

She ducked down, expecting to hear gunfire. The street was quiet. She turned onto Pennsylvania Avenue, passing a gas station, a Kinko's, and neighborhood restaurants. She drove by the Library of Congress, a colossal white structure, and the U.S. Capitol, lit with yellow lights against the dark sky. As she neared the Justice Department, she checked her rearview mirror. The large boulevard was nearly empty. Where are they? She drove into the parking lot. There were a few parked cars in the dark lot. There were no people. She wasn't sure if that was a good thing or a bad thing. Taking a deep breath, she jumped out of the car and sprinted around the building. She banged on the thick glass double doors. A heavy-eyed security guard rose. He smiled when he recognized her face. He fumbled with the lock, opening the doors. She glanced over her shoulder. Men were racing toward her. She pushed past the security guard, slamming the doors shut. Surprised, the security guard asked, "Are you all right, Ms. Cox?"

"No, Fred. I'm not all right." Standing behind him, she peered out the doors. The men vanished.

The security guard followed her gaze. His eyebrows were knitted; he was perplexed.

"Lock these doors and don't let anyone else in," said Sidney, breathing deeply.

"No problem," he said.

"Is Deputy Director Thomas in?"

"Yes, madam," he said.

Passing by the mosaic walls of the lobby, Sidney stopped at the elevator bank. What had just happened? Who were those men? That had been a narrow escape. She needed to get to a phone to warn Michael. And Damian. Who else needed to know? She stepped into the empty elevator and pressed the button for the top floor. As the elevator rose, she watched the white light pass the sixth and seventh floors. Feeling drained, Sidney leaned against a brown panel wall. She touched her forehead. It was damp. She took two deep breaths.

The lights in the elevator dimmed. Sidney blinked twice. What was that? The elevator suddenly dropped a floor. Her stomach flew up. *Oh, my God.* The lights flickered. *Oh, my God.* The lights came back on. She exhaled. The elevator dropped again. The lights went off. Sidney screamed as the elevator fell.

THE LYING THIEF

CHAPTER 7

Late Thursday night. "We found medetomidine mixed with
ketamine on a cot outside of Bogotá, Colombia," said
Charles Thomas. The Deputy Director glanced around the Justice
Department conference room. When he had returned to his own
office, after Shannon's untimely departure, an interesting message
had been waiting for him. He had placed calls to Sidney Cox and
Damian Stagel, but they had not arrived yet. He had sent an agent
to find them over an hour ago.

"Was that the same sedative found in Alexander's blood?" asked
Martinez, the DEA head.

Thomas glanced down at a DNA report and flipped it open.
"The same sedative. And the same blood."

"There's a match?"

"An exact match." Thomas paused, thinking about the
Colombia raid. They had been lucky to find this connection, but
he couldn't help wishing his men had arrived sooner at the drug
factory. "Roger Alexander is still alive," said Thomas. "And he is—
or was—somewhere outside of Bogotá."

Silence.

"That's a strong sedative, right?" asked Martinez. "An animal
tranquillizer, you said?" asked Paul Martinez.

"Yes, it slows the pulse, the heartbeat and causes shortness of
breath in large animals, like horses, lions—"

"What are the chances that Alexander survived the tranquilizer?"

"Don't know. It causes vomiting in dogs and cats. And abortions
in cattle, but God only knows what it will do to Roger Alexander."

"Then what are the chances that he survived Andres Santos?"

An hour later, Charles Thomas walked back into the conference room. The team was busy working. He beckoned to Paul Martinez. They stepped out into the hallway. "Ana Santos has been extradited and will arrive in the United States tonight," said Thomas.

"That's good," said Martinez. "So why do you look like someone just ran over your pet turtle?"

The door shut behind them. Thomas stepped closer to Martinez. "They're gone," he said.

"What do you mean?" asked Martinez.

"All three of them are gone. Without a trace."

"You spoke with Michael Hollander and Danielle Sanchez?"

"They spent the evening with Damian and Sidney," said Thomas. "Both got my call on their cell phones and then they left to come here." Thomas cracked his knuckles. "Sidney's car is parked in the lot. Or rather Michael's Lexus. The rear bumper is dented up pretty good."

"Anything else?"

"He says his pistol is missing."

"Pistol?"

"He's a criminal defense lawyer," said Thomas, shrugging his shoulders. "You never know."

"Anything else?"

"Wendy's green car is smashed up." Thomas cleared his throat. "It was in the lot, too."

"What about Wendy?"

Charles slid a hand into his pocket. "I may have been the last person to see her . . ." He fingered her red security badge in his pocket.

"Did you hear back from anyone?" asked Martinez. "I mean, before . . ."

"I got a voicemail from Sidney. Right after she and I spoke—"

"What did she say?"

"Remember the term one of the fake paramedics used?"

Martinez shook his head. "No, I thought you weren't quite sure . . ."

"Sidney figured it out," said Thomas. He trusted her. Her Spanish was fluent, having spent a time overseas and she had confirmed it with a staffer. Besides, he and a naval buddy had a short assignment down there. "It's used by *sicarios*. A Colombian slang term."

They both knew sicarios were teenager killers for hire in Colombia. They were cheap, dependable killers that eliminated rivals, cheats and informers. They used their own vocabulary and jargon to code their conversations.

"What was the term?" asked Martinez, beginning to look uneasy.

"*Borror los testigos.*"

Together they said, "To get rid of witnesses."

———————————

Friday first light. Sitting on the floor, they watched and waited. Eyes closed and panting for air, she finally raised her head. Her tongue slid over her dry lips. She raised a hand to her head and grimaced. She appeared grimy and hot. Opening one eye, she blinked several times as if her vision was blurry. They checked for a pulse. It was faint. She lay back down and they groaned. After several minutes, Wendy Shannon opened both eyes.

Sidney and Damian returned her gaze. Finally, she frowned. They frowned back.

"Another fine mess you've gotten us into," said Damian, scowling at the U.S. Attorney.

Looking around, Shannon took a deep breath. "What makes you think this is my fault?"

"History. Common sense," said Damian. "Your presence."

Shannon glanced at Sidney.

"I'm with him," said Sidney as her eyes narrowed.

"Figures," said Shannon, crossing her arms.

Sidney studied Shannon. Her gray suit was grimy, her forehead was scraped, but she looked none the worse for wear. Her breathing was returning to normal and her gray eyes were focused. Sidney glanced at Damian. He stretched out his long body. His jeans were torn at the knees; the elbows of his jacket covered in grass stains. His knees and elbows had been skinned while ramming into a motorcycle and getting shoved out of a cab. She had not gotten all the details behind the taxi episode yet, but she had gotten the general gist. And frankly, she was as surprised as hell to discover that she was still alive after her little fall from grace. The elevator had stopped short of crashing. She had slammed into a wall. The next thing she knew she was waking up in a narrow, bricked-in crawlspace. She had been held there all alone for hours. Later, she woke up across from Damian. Her vision had been blurry and her breathing shallow. However, as far as she could discern, she only had a backache that made her wish she was dead, dying or something far worse.

Earlier, Sidney had managed to glance out a window. She had spotted guards and what appeared to be an electrified fence. From somewhere in the house, she thought she heard a private elevator. She later heard helicopter blades and glimpsed a midnight blue helicopter darting across the hazy skyline. She wondered what kind of colonial mansion had a helipad on its rooftop.

Sidney glanced back at Shannon as her gray eyes passed over the room—a tasteful living room. The large house was filled with seventeenth-century antiques, dramatic paintings and handmade crafts, including a few pre-Colombian ceramic pieces.

"Where are we?" asked Shannon. Her voice was scratchy; her eyebrows gathered.

"Welcome to Bogotá," said Sidney.

Automatic weapons locked and cocked around them.

Friday first light. "We're targeting three suspects," said Charles Thomas. "Roger Alexander. Andres Santos. And Christina Savant."

"Why them?" asked Paul Martinez, the DEA head.

"Why these three hostages?" asked Thomas. "Sidney Cox. Damian Stagel. Wendy Shannon." Thomas scanned the large room. He could feel the fear in the silent conference room. Each member of the Task Force wondered if she would be next. After all, someone had shot the Police Chief through the heart. "There's overlap." Thomas paused. "We're looking for means, motive, and opportunity."

Silence.

"First, Roger Alexander is either the mastermind or the victim here," said Thomas. "He either escaped or was kidnapped. Either way, he is our number one suspect. Second, Andres Santos is possibly the drug connection behind the murder of the Attorney General. The blood on the cot connects the Santos cartel to Roger Alexander. We shut down a division of his operation and we have his sister in lock-up. Third, Christina Savant has a grand jury hearing on Monday. If her company is indicted, Christina loses everything."

Thomas had retrieved an FBI file from Sidney's office. He had reviewed Christina Savant's work history. He had been surprised that she had spent ten years working for a competitor of CSC, running its South American division. Apparently, she had been kicking butt, because her brother had lured her away to run his South American division. However, she had later been demoted, down to the Bogotá subsidiary.

"If this is connected to Colombia," said Martinez, "then we better get to Sidney and the others fast. Kidnapping down there is a sophisticated business. Kidnappers collected more than two hundred and fifty million dollars in ransom payments last year." Martinez leaned forward. "It's bad down there."

Earlier, Martinez had briefed Thomas on his contacts down in Colombia. Martinez had called several Colombian newspapers. Editors were regularly threatened; their phones tapped; their relatives trailed; and their offices bombed. In the last five years, twenty-three journalists had been killed while reporting aggressively against the cocaine cartels. The owners of one newspaper could no longer buy life insurance, so they had forty bodyguards on the payroll and owned six armored cars.

"Maybe the drug lords are exporting kidnapping along with the drugs," said Thomas. He paused as he met the frightened stares in the room. "Let's get tight surveillance for each member of the Task Force and for the families of the hostages." He drummed his pen on a note pad. "I want Bruce Lewis moved to maximum security. In fact, let's pay the attorney a visit."

"Did you have me kidnapped?" asked Shannon, looking disgusted.

"Oh, get over yourself," said Damian.

Stepping out of the cool house into the humidity, ahead of the other two, Sidney said, "Can we all just get along—at least until they shoot us?"

Seated in the backseat of a jeep, at gunpoint, they rode out of an upscale neighborhood. Without turning her head, Sidney had heard other engines start and follow. Inhaling exhaust fumes, she watched as they passed a major hospital, an international hotel and an office complex. Riding through the center of town, Sidney saw speeding convoys of bullet-proof SUVs and motorcycle chase teams. Soldiers patrolled outside government buildings, elegant shopping centers, futuristic glass towers, and luxury apartment buildings. Homes and corporate headquarters were ringed by steel fences; armed guards were everywhere.

They drove through the streets heading north, passing the downtown area. It became seedier. Then they turned and headed out of the city, passing open-air bargaining markets and colonial churches. In the surrounding hills, Sidney could see shanties. However, dense fog obscured the skyline, a panoramic view from Rio Bogotá to the colonial city.

"Where are we?" asked Shannon.

"Not now," said Sidney, keeping an eye on the armed men. Squeezed between the others, she began to perspire in the scorching heat. She regretted her decision to change into black clothes. She was feeling sticky, especially pressed up against Shannon's light wool suit. The only thing that made her feel a bit better was knowing that Shannon was about to liquefy. She glanced at her face. It was a light shade of pink.

"Where—" started Shannon.

"We're in North Bogotá," said Sidney.

"That's just great," said Shannon, wiping the sweat from her forehead.

They rode along rugged unpaved roads, stopping only once, to refuel. As the yellowish-orange sun descended, six or seven hours later, the jeep pulled up to a small white house in the countryside. The men, wearing camouflage uniforms, led the three up a hill into a green pasture, where they waited. The air was damp, thin and very cold.

Shivering in the great outdoors, Sidney was feeling better about her clothing choice. She glanced around and then into the eyes of Damian Stagel. She whispered, "We're in real trouble here."

"I know," said Damian, looking concerned.

"What's going on?" asked Shannon, stepping closer to the others.

"We're friends now?" whispered Damian.

"We need to work together," said Shannon, pulling her suit jacket tightly around her.

"How can you help us?" asked Damian. "You don't even know where you are."

"Our lives are in danger and you're holding some petty grudge?" asked Shannon.

"You tried to have us executed," said Damian.

"That was ages ago."

"That was this summer."

"What's a teeny mistake amongst friends?" asked Shannon hopefully.

"What—" said Damian, stepping closer to her.

Shannon stepped backwards. "I'll scream," said Shannon.

"Who wouldn't?" said Damian, stepping closer.

"We think we're at Camino del Secuestro,'" said Sidney.

"Where is that?" asked Shannon, keeping an anxious eye on the retreating Damian.

"It's called the Kidnap Trail," said Sidney, glancing around. She spotted the armed men standing at a distance near a wooded area. She looked up. Was that a plane in the distance? She could not be sure.

"Details, please?" asked Shannon, placing her hands on her thick hips.

"It leads into the mountain of Sumapaz," said Sidney. She had spent time in Bogotá during school and later on, business, but she had never been outside the city. However, she thought she recognized this place from news reports. "It's a rebel stronghold, south of Bogotá."

"You mean we've been kidnapped by rebels?" asked Shannon.

"I don't know," said Sidney. "Down here it's hard to say. They've got left-wing guerrilla groups . . . right-wing paramilitaries. These folks have been at war for forty years." The spot in the sky that might have been a plane had faded into grayish-white clouds.

"Like I didn't have enough troubles of my own," said Shannon, pushing her glasses up.

"Maybe they're waiting to take us to La Casa de La O," said Sidney. "A farmhouse where they keep kidnapped victims. "It's where they receive family members who track out from Bogotá to negotiate releases."

"They come all the way out here to drop off ransoms?" asked Shannon.

"Yep," said Damian, leaning over her. "Anybody coming for you?"

Shannon blinked twice.

Deep in thought, Sidney ignored them. Last week, she had helped the FBI Director finalize an upcoming Presidential announcement. This country was the central piece of that strategy. The President wanted to stem the flow of illegal drugs from ᵐbia, the source of nearly all cocaine used in the United States. ʳd-nosed policies of the Colombian President had reduced ᵗion of coca, the main ingredient of cocaine, by fifteen ʳ he needed help. President Wright had stepped in, a grace period to switch from coca to legal crops.

After that, he had ordered U.S.-funded aerial herbicide sprayings, destroying hundreds of thousands of acres of illegal crops. Now, he wanted to do more.

However, because drug money and kidnappings funded the rebels, Colombia also reigned as the world leader in kidnappings. Three thousand people were kidnapped here each year. In the past two months, a presidential candidate, a Colombian senator and a former culture minister had been kidnapped and killed. Nearly ten thousand families were waiting for a wife, a cousin, a mother or a father to return; thousands more simply disappeared. Despite economic problems, including a twenty-percent unemployment rate, a two-billion-dollar-a-year security industry thrived in Colombia. Colombians were armoring and bullet-proofing more than two thousand cars a year. Plastic surgeons had produced a cottage industry of treating wealthy victims who returned from kidnappings with sliced ears, severed fingers and other missing body parts that had been sent to wives, husbands or children as threats for ransom payments. Somehow, the second oldest democracy in the Western Hemisphere was engaged in the longest-running civil war in history. Despite a three-year peace process, there were six kidnappings per day. Where they half of today's quota?

"But it could be the drug lords," said Damian, interrupting Sidney's thoughts.

"Friends of yours?" asked Shannon.

Damian narrowed his eyes.

Shannon backed up.

Stepping between them, Sidney said, "Do you think they injected us with that animal tranquilizer? The kind they shot into Roger Alexander?"

THE INQUISITION

CHAPTER 8

F riday midmorning. Six hours earlier. They entered the silent maximum-security unit. Flanked by Paul Martinez and a brigade of FBI agents, Charles Thomas moved swiftly down the corridor. His eyes scanned the unit. At the far end, a cell was isolated and well guarded. As they drew near it, a thin guard, in a baggy gray uniform, unlocked the thick steel door and then stood clear. They entered the cell, a ten-by-twelve cement box.

Bruce Lewis sat on the lower bunk bed, staring at a cider block wall. His ash blond hair lay against his damp forehead. Pink splotches spotted his pale cheeks. He ran his hand through his thin hair. His hand dropped to his lap and began picking at his orange jumpsuit. Lynnwood Correctional Facility was stamped across the back. Two days ago, Roger Alexander had been sitting in this very spot. Now, he was long gone.

"Why can't I see my wife and sons?" asked Bruce. They had been allowed only one visit.

"What's the connection between Andres Santos and Christina Savant?" asked Thomas, looming over the chief counsel for CSC.

Bruce blinked rapidly. "Is it true that Ana Santos was extradited?"

"She arrived an hour ago," said Thomas, raising an eyebrow. On the way here, they had stopped by the cell of Ana Santos. She had been charged with cocaine trafficking, attempted murder, illegal arms possession and organized crime. As a result, she was quite taken with her new right to remain silent.

"Is the amnesty deal still on the table?" asked Bruce. He locked eyes with the Deputy Director. "You'll let me just walk away."

"Yes," said Thomas. "Instead of facing an indictment on drug trafficking charges and spending what's left of your life in prison, you could simply walk away. With your family."

"This is killing me," said Bruce quietly. "I can't pick up my boys. I need to hold them. They must be asking for me." His bluish-gray eyes reddened. "I need them." Tears rimmed his eyes.

Thomas recalled his visit to the Police Chief's widow. Childless, she had been sitting alone, surrounded by dishes of food from friends. As tears formed in her eyes, he had offered to accompany her to the funeral. Grateful, her tears had refused to fall.

Bruce cleared his throat and his tears receded. "I'll tell you whatever you want to know." He took a deep breath. "But here's the deal," he said. "No jail time. No monetary fine. Witness protection for me and my family. And a flight to a non-extraditable country."

"Done," said Thomas. "What do you know?"

"I know where the laptop is," said Bruce.

Silence.

Waiting, Thomas held his breath. The laptop had been missing since the day Roger Alexander shot himself. The FBI Director had set it down as they had all lunged for Alexander who was pointing his pistol at Sidney. Fortunately, the pistol had swung, the bullet piercing Peter Savant. However, Alexander's laptop had disappeared in the commotion. "Go on," said Thomas.

"The one with the financial records linking the Santos cartel and CSC. Dates. Dollar amounts. Shipments."

Thomas exhaled slowly. "Do you want to wait for your lawyer?"

"No. And you can tell him I said that," said Bruce.

"You can tell me yourself," said Nathaniel Drake, trailed by two young associates from Drake, Spaulding & Lloyd.

Disappointment washed over Thomas as he stepped away from the door allowing the attorney to enter the cell.

Drake glanced around. "What's going on here?"

"Ask your client," said Thomas.

"Do you mind waiting outside?" asked Bruce, looking at his lawyer.

"Christina Savant is paying your legal bills and she wants me here," said Drake.

"This will only take a minute," said Bruce.

"That's what concerns me," said Drake.

"Although she pays you," said Bruce, "and although we're colleagues, you work for me. Please step outside." Bruce stared up at his partner. Before this fiasco, Bruce had been the biggest rainmaker at Drake, Spaulding & Lloyd, bringing in millions of dollars in fees from CSC. Greed had been his downfall.

Nathaniel met his stare. "This interview is over." He paused. "Your wife would not want this."

Bruce looked away first. He bowed his head. "This interview is over," said Bruce.

———————

Later that morning, Thomas sat alone in the Justice Department conference room. He had a meeting in ten minutes. While he waited for his target to arrive, he thought about Bruce. If Bruce wanted protection for his family, he would have to ask for it. There was nothing Thomas could do about veiled threats. He exhaled, thinking about the hostages. Thomas was deeply troubled about Sidney and the others. *How was Wendy holding up?* he wondered. *Was she driving the other two insane?* The crazy person in the room always thought she was the sanest person in the room. He smiled and then it faded. He had been in constant contact with Danielle Sanchez and Michael Hollander about Sidney and Damian. Thomas clenched his jaw.

To occupy his thoughts, he flipped opened a FBI file. It was the second file that he had retrieved from Sidney's office. It had been lying near the one he had claimed last night. In this one, a black-and-white photo was stapled to the inside of the brown manila folder. He examined the photo. On the other side of the folder, pages were filled with information regarding the target.

Gender: Female. Age: 34. Alias: None. Immediate family: Father, Mother and Brother—All Deceased. Education: Secondary Education—Phillips Exeter Academy. Undergraduate: Sorbonne, Paris, France. Magna cum laude. Graduate Degree: Masters of Business Administration, New York University. Language Fluency: Spanish, Arabic, Portuguese, French, English. The file contained no information about a lover, boyfriend or husband.

Thomas glanced up, thinking. He stared at the mural on the east wall. He studied a satanic man holding an angelic mask. He flipped open the second file. As he scanned it, a smile crossed his lips. He realized again that Sidney was a clever girl. There was a reason she had both files lying open, side by side. He sat in the conference room, thinking and waiting.

Ten minutes later, he stared into the emerald eyes of Christina Savant. Her perfume drifted in the air. Seated on the other side of the oval table, she wore a fitted green business suit that matched her eyes. She flipped her long red hair and locked eyes with him. He detected no fear in her eyes, unlike Bruce. Her attorney sat quietly at her side, looking courtly and docile.

"Three members of this Task Force are missing," said Thomas. "And a convicted murderer is on the run. What do you know about that?"

"Nothing."

Thomas studied her. She had looked neither right nor left. Thomas knew the brain stored information in different areas causing a person to look to the right to retrieve a memory, but left to think of an answer. "Did you introduce Ana Santos to your brother, Peter Savant?" He watched her eyes and her body language.

Before answering, she straightened her skirt and crossed her legs. "Is that what Ana told you?"

"How did you know Ana was in custody?"

Thinking, she looked to the left. "I'm sure it's been in the newspaper."

"Which newspaper?"

"Am I under suspicion for a particular crime?" asked Ms. Savant.

"Did your brother demote you because you brought a drug cartel into his company?"

"I was demoted for personal reasons. Not business reasons, Mr. Thomas."

"What personal reasons?"

"None of your business," said Christina, holding up a manicured hand as her lawyer leaned forward.

"When did you first meet Ana Santos? At Phillips Exeter Academy or down in the Village at New York University?"

Looking left again, Christina hesitated. "I don't recall."

"Where were you Wednesday afternoon?"

"At the office."

"All afternoon?"

"All afternoon," she said.

"Where were you last night?" asked Thomas.

"At the office," said Christina, raising her chin. "All night."

He slid a document across the desk to her lawyer.

Drake picked it up. "What's this?"

"It's a subpoena. I want all her phone records. For work, for home, and for her cell phone. Agents should be arriving at her office—" Thomas glanced at his watch, "right about now. They'll be confirming your alibi," he said, gazing at her.

"Are you accusing the CEO of CSC of kidnapping federal officials and helping Roger Alexander escape?" asked Drake.

"What makes you think he escaped?" asked Thomas.

"Kidnapped, escaped, murdered, whatever," said Drake, flipping open a cell phone. He stood up, turned his back, and spoke quickly into the phone. He closed the phone and sat down.

"When was the last time you were in Colombia, Ms. Savant?" asked Thomas.

"Four months ago."

Thomas slid another document to her lawyer. "I want your passport surrendered—today."

"You can't do that," said Drake.
"Take it up with Judge Lombard."

—————————

Wet and cold, the three hostages were forced through a densely wooded area. The air had grown cooler as they headed up the mountains. After several hours, they approached a large rectangular building. Armed guards patrolled the area. Security cameras watched. From the tin roof, deep dish satellites listened.

Sidney glanced twice at the man standing at the door. Both his head and hand were bandaged tightly. He glared at them. A .357 Magnum was down at his side. Both Sidney and Shannon glanced away. After issuing instructions quickly in Spanish, the bandaged man took them into the building. To Sidney, it looked like a large laboratory or a factory. It smelled of alcohol and ammonia. Men and women stood behind long tables. Their mouths and noses were covered with white masks and they wore white lab coats. On the tables was an assortment of items. Sidney glanced at Damian as his eyes absorbed the activities in the cavernous room. His dark eyes filled with regret.

In an instant, Damian recognized the blue glassing bags used to package heroin. Traditional balloons were no longer in vogue for China White, a street name for heroin. The workers removed gum from green opium poppy capsules, extracted morphine from the gum and then converted the morphine into heroin. The chemical reaction required a variety of solvents, additives and alkaline including lime, ammonia, and tartaric acid as well as alcohol and acetone. Damian assumed the dark bottles contained those substances.

Seven tables over, clear containers of white crystalline powder stood next to liters of ethyl ether, acetone, ammonia, sulphuric acid and hydrochloric acid. Several tables over from the cocaine, Damian noticed large chunky clear crystals resembling rock candy. Crystal Meth or Ice could be smoked like crack cocaine. About 10 to 15 hits could be taken from a single gram of the stuff. It was a

toxic, addictive stimulant. Ecstasy—E, Fantasy, Lover's Speed—
was in the packages with the butterfly logs. The drug caused sensual
arousal. Damian knew it also caused nausea, blurred vision,
depression, as well as kidney failure and permanent brain damage.

After they crossed the factory floor, the short bandaged man
leaned close to an optical reader—small and black with a numbered
keypad. A light passed over his eye, identifying him by reading his
retina. The door to a large office opened. Three of the walls were
made of glass. He directed them to enter. The thick door snapped
shut behind them.

Through the glass, Sidney could see the full factory floor
and hundreds of factory workers. She also saw armed men
watching her. The men turned, busy with some other matter.
Feeling grimy, hungry and drained, she turned around, checking
the room. A large television sat in the corner, mute but turned
to an international station for CNN. A weatherman smiled and
vanished. Photos of their three faces appeared. Their faces
vanished. Charles Thomas appeared, flapping his arms in
frustration in the middle of a chaotic scene outside the
courthouse. He vanished and a commercial came on. Sidney
turned. They were alone with a desk and chair; several
computers, including a gray laptop; a computer-generated wall
map; and lot of technical equipment.

From DEA briefings, Sidney knew drug traffickers had the
best technology that money could buy. They had billions of dollars
and no rules on how to spend it. While the government was required
to bid out contracts, cartels purchased state-of-the-art technology,
including spy satellites, AWACS, and radar surveillance planes.
They could intercept telephone calls, set up electronic surveillance,
and encrypt their own cellular phone calls. They even hired former
intelligence officers from a variety of countries to operate the
equipment.

Shannon stepped forward, staring at the computers. One was
turned on.

Sidney glanced at the monitor. It was a remote video
monitoring system. It was exactly like the one that she had seen at

DEA. It probably allowed them to dial up and view from 16 different camera angles any of their factories. Sidney doubted that they saved any of these panoramic views on the hard drives of their computers. If they did, it would be too easy for someone to take it. Her eyes passed over the computer-generated wall map, stopped and returned. She recognized the locations of several blinking markers.

Grabbing Shannon's arm as she moved toward one of the computers, Damian nodded upward at a smoke detector.

"It's a smoke alarm. So what?" asked Shannon, stopping in her tracks.

"It's a fully functional, high-resolution, solid state CCD camera," said Damian. "That's what."

Shannon patted her jacket pocket. "I bet you two would be a lot nicer to me if you knew I had a satellite cell phone."

They stopped, turned and stared at her.

Shannon smiled back.

The door unlocked and swung open. A man entered. He had neatly trimmed black hair, a narrow face, ginger skin, dark eyes, and wore an expensive black suit. He sat behind a large brown desk. He reached across the neat desk and turned off the computer. The bandaged man walked into the room. He nudged the three captives into chairs in front of the desk.

Sitting, Sidney ignored the bandaged man, staring at the other man behind the desk. She leaned forward. "I know who you are," she said.

"I know who I am, too," he said. "Now what?"

"I was wondering," said Shannon, "Mr.—"

"Andres Santos," he said.

"Mr. Santos," said Shannon, "Were you planning on committing any rapes or assaults this morning?"

Damian and Sidney turned to stare at her.

He chuckled. "You're asking me if I'm going to assault you," said Andres. "Look at what you've done to my people."

They glanced out the glass walls. Men stood all around, all bandaged up.

"I've got burnt hands," said Andres. "A run-over foot. A maced eye. A dented head. A piece of an ear. Ask my cousin." He flipped his hand.

They glanced at the man with the bandaged head. The cousin glared. Sidney looked away.

"That shot was an inch away from being fatal." He looked at his men and then at his three captives. "Shit."

Silence.

"Besides, I'm not trying to die out here, Ms. Shannon," said Andres. "I have a wife and two daughters. If I raped you, the police would never find my body parts."

"I was just wondering," said Shannon.

Andres's eyebrows gathered as he looked at the prosecutor. He frowned and then turned his attention to Damian. "How many kids do you and your wife have?"

"None," said Damian. "I'm not married."

"Really?" asked Andres. He turned to Sidney. "You?"

"No."

He looked at Shannon. "You?"

Silence.

"What the hell are you people waiting on?"

His cell phone rang. He pulled it out of his suit pocket, glanced at the phone number of the caller and said, "Excuse me." He answered it in Spanish. He glanced at Sidney. She averted her eyes. Well educated and polished, he switched to French. His voice rose. Appearing agitated, Andres Santos stood and left the room. His cousin followed him out the door. It snapped shut.

Shannon slapped her forehead. "What in the hell have I been doing for the last forty-two years? The Colombian drug lord has a more functional life than I do. He's got a wife, two kids, a house, probably a dog and even steaks in the refrigerator. Jesus."

Damian glared at her with narrowed eyes. "Wonder if he has a decanter of hemlock?"

"What is your problem?" said Shannon. "I was just saying—"

"Hey, hey, hey," said Sidney. "You're like two old winos sitting on a railroad track."

"Well, I have feelings, too, you know," sulked Shannon.

"What was that about a cell phone?" asked Sidney. "And why didn't you mention it before?"

"This is the first time we've been alone," said Shannon. "Sort of."

"Were you planning on leaving here without us?" asked Damian.

Sidney raised an eyebrow.

"I forgot about it, okay?" said Shannon.

"You forgot about it, my ass," said Damian.

"Whatever," said Sidney. She wondered if Thomas had linked the Santoses to Christina Savant yet. When she had pulled their FBI files, she thought she remembered some connection. It had been the schools. She had not had a chance to tell anyone. "Will it work from here?" Sidney looked intensely at Shannon.

"Yes," said Shannon. "No. Yes."

"Focus because I need clarity," said Sidney.

The office door opened.

Andres Santos entered. "Enough chitchat. Where is my sister?"

———

In Arlington Cemetery, under a gray sky, Thomas stood silently next to David Warden's widow. Among the thousands of white headstones, hundreds of friends had arrived at the burial site of the Police Chief. Even more people, the FBI Director and the President, had attended the funeral service at a large church in Northwest Washington. As Thomas watched, a flag was presented to the widow and the coffin was lowered into the damp ground.

Thomas recommitted himself to solving this case. David was dead. Three hostages were kidnapped. Roger Alexander had vanished. The media would not give him a moment's peace. And his mind would not stop racing. It focused on Andres Santos. The man was responsible for shipping nearly a quarter of the cocaine consumed in the U.S. last year. He was one of Colombia's most powerful drug dealers. He was wanted on 20 charges, including drug trafficking, money laundering and murder. He also had a habit of shooting his victims through the heart.

Thomas thought about the night Ana Santos had been captured. Her arrest had been caught on film, by the Santoses' own security cameras. Large black helicopters had swarmed the long narrow compound, landing on the roof, out in the woods, and in front of the building. FBI and DEA agents had smashed through the front gates with wrecking equipment. Everyone inside had been taken by surprise. Young men and women were running everywhere. The agents had been on their bullhorns, shouting, "Halt!" They had strict orders to shoot only in self-defense. Colombian forces had shattered the front door. They began arresting people.

Along with her two body guards, Ana Santos was snagged as she dashed out the back door and launched her petite frame over a fence. An agent grabbed her by the shirt, in mid-air. Twenty minutes later, she was in handcuffs and on her way to Bogotá. At first, she had remained calmed, joking with Colombian police.

However, by the time Ana reached the capital, the President of Colombia had already signed an extradition order. Ana was hustled to the Bogotá airport. She was quickly handed over to the FBI and DEA. When she realized she was headed to the United States, she lost her composure. Agents had to drag her from an armored van and hoist her up the steps into a military jet. While seated in the aircraft, she stared at the 20 FBI agents surrounding her. "You are all dead men," she said.

For the past three years, she had distributed drugs in dozens of American cities, earning as much as $1.5 billion a year. She and her brother had spent millions of those dollars bribing judges, police officials and even cabinet members. While those payments had rendered them invincible during the former Colombian administration, it now made them dangerous. A list of bribed public officials could cause a scandal. It had led to her hasty departure.

Thomas knew drug dealing ultimately led to money laundering. What to do with all that money? Thomas had the Task Force tracking the money. Ana's job, facilitated by her business degree, had been to clean up the money. She knew if and when trucks carrying loads of money crossed U.S. southern borders; if and when deposits were made into the treasury of CSC, perhaps through its Bogotá subsidiary; if and when dollars were wired to Cayman Island holding companies; and if and when that cleaned-up cash was invested in real estate, computer stores, car dealerships and meat-packing plants from here to Switzerland.

Thomas had felt certain they would capture the Santoses. They had both made the roster of the FBI's Ten Most Wanted List six months ago. Since 1950, nearly all of the 500 most-wanted fugitives had been caught. Started under J. Edgar Hoover, nearly half had been nabbed due to snitching and rewards. As soon as they released the news of the capture, Ana Santos would remain on the list for a few weeks with a red captured tag slashed across her face. Thomas often explained to new recruits that it was like having a "Sold" sign on a house. It was good advertising.

Besides, Ana was unique; she was one of only seven women who had ever joined the elite fraternity. Today, the Top Ten were mostly men, suspected of terrorism, murder or drug dealing. However, the characteristics changed from decade to decade. In the 1950s, the list consisted of robbers and car thieves. In the '60s and '70s, it was saboteurs and ideological radicals. However, when a police officer or an FBI agent was murdered, the stakes went up. The reward for Andres Santos and Roger Alexander had skyrocketed from two million dollars to twenty-five million dollars each.

As he stepped away from the gravesite, Thomas thought about Ana's replacement on the list. Where was Roger Alexander?

The long black limousine glided through the streets of New York. Departing La Guardia Airport, it had crossed the Manhattan Bridge into the city. Once in Manhattan, it pulled up to a thirty-five-story, silver skyscraper on Park Avenue. Savant Plaza was inscribed in elegant black letters above three revolving glass doors. Christina Savant slid out of the vehicle, entered the cathedral vestibule, strode by ceiling-high palm trees and rode the elevator to the receptionist's area on the thirty-fourth floor.

The receptionist, elegantly dressed, smiled pleasantly. "Welcome, Ms. Savant." She sat behind a large round oak wood receptionist desk. Exquisite French impressionist paintings adorned the rich maroon walls. "I hope you had a pleasant flight."

Christina nodded. "Amanda."

"They are waiting for you in the conference room," said the receptionist. "We've prepared light refreshments for your meeting."

"Thank you," said Christina, turning on high heels. She entered the conference room. Seated on the other side of the mahogany table, in front of heavy white drapes, sat a battery of attorneys from Drake, Spaulding & Lloyd. After she sat down at the head of the table, they explained their partial success. They had been able to limit the search. FBI agents had interrogated the staff and search the offices; however, they had been forced to retreat from a search of the penthouse residence. Nevertheless, they would be back.

Christina dismissed the attorneys. She walked down the hallway to a private elevator, punched in a security code and rode the elevator up to the penthouse. When the elevator doors slid open, she stepped into an enormous office with three glass walls. It was a breathtaking view of the entire length of Manhattan, from the George Washington Bridge, above 179th Street, down to the tip of the island, below 1st street. A Renoir painting hung on the fourth wall.

She crossed to the far end of the room and sat behind a hand-carved, Chinese red antique desk. Behind her, a wall was covered with citations, awards and plaques from the city fathers honoring her brother's philanthropy. She thought about him. Ten years older, Peter Savant had been disciplined power. He had lifted weights from 4:00 A.M. to 6:00 A.M. seven days a week before starting his seventeen-hour workdays. All five feet, eleven inches, and two hundred pounds of him had been muscular curves and smooth surfaces. At forty-five, he had been a hard-charging workaholic who slept in a room just up the spiral staircase. His mansion in Greenwich, Connecticut; cottage in the Blue Ridge Mountains; and villa in the French Rivera were usually empty. Women and children had been mere distractions. He hadn't taken a vacation in ten years. Peter Savant had been a self-made millionaire on his way to billionaire status.

Christina reached across his desk and picked up an old-fashioned black-and-white photograph in a pewter frame. She gazed at their father's face. It was a picture of an elegantly dressed, older man sitting in front of a small white house. There was nothing unusual about the man, except for his eyes. They were vacant. He appeared lost. Pierre Savant had been a French diplomat. He had traveled the globe. His children had attended the best schools and had been treated like royalty. But her brother had seen him as a weak man when he had made bad investments and worse friends. Her father had lost everything. They had been evicted from their home in Paris, reduced to living in a small house out in the countryside. Their father had died a drunk.

When she discovered the photograph in the desk drawer, she had been surprised. Peter had paid for her education, but had otherwise kept his distance from the family and from her. She set it down on the far end of his desk.

She thought about their last conversation. Unlike hers, his English has been flawless, without a trace of a French accent. He had excelled at everything. Was that the reason she hated him so? Or was it that he had abandoned his family to poverty? Or was it that he had finally hired her and then humiliated her?

Peter Savant had been arrogant. He had not listened to her. And he had not listened to his Chief Financial Officer. His Colombian subsidiary was going under for the last count. Losing money faster than he could keep count. It could take the entire company down. The CFO had pressed his point over and over until Savant had whirled on him during a meeting, screaming at him. It had shaken the CFO. By the time he raised the issue again, it was too late. By that time, Savant was desperate. The company was deeply in debt. The banks were calling in loans. Entering the CFO's office late one night, Savant had suggested he change a few entries in the company's financial ledgers. Who would ever know? The CFO had refused. Far less egregious acts had torched powerhouse Enron, including its CFO. So, Savant doubled the CFO's six-figure salary. The CFO changed the entries.

Later, Peter Savant had hired his sister, tricked her, watched her take desperate measures, blamed her for the mess, and then demoted her. The problem only mushroomed when the CFO, working long hours, stressed out and no longer taking his lithium, got himself arrested, charged and locked up with rapists, murderers, and all-purpose lunatics. To protect himself, he had copied incriminating financial records. Now, he was dead, hanged in his jail cell, and the rest of them were following in his wake.

She crossed the office and flipped open her new cell phone. She began climbing a circular staircase to the residential quarters. She dialed a number, waited for an answer, and began speaking in Spanish into the tiny phone.

"How's your sister?" asked Christina.

"How's your brother?" asked Andres Santos.

"When you see him, be sure to ask him."

"I heard you've been talking to the FBI."

She paused on the staircase. "Why are they asking me questions about you?"

"Care to expound?"

"I'm not a messenger," she said.

"They think I'm working with you," said Andres.

"That's rich." She moved up the staircase. "Bruce Lewis is cutting a deal with the feds," said Christina.

Silence.

"Are you there?" asked Christina.

"What about you?" asked Andres.

"What about you?" asked Christina.

They listened to each other breathe.

"Is Ana talking to the FBI?" asked Christina.

"Does that mean you don't have her?" asked Andres.

Christina paused on the staircase again. "Maybe I do and maybe I don't."

"We've been friends for a long time," said Andres. His voice was tinged with anger. "We should trust each other more than this."

"Ana and I are friends," said Christina, "You, on the other hand, are a lying thief."

"I don't remember lying," said Andres.

"Where's my laptop?" asked Christina.

"Where's Roger Alexander?"

"You've got some nerve," said Christina.

"Oh, I get it," said Andres. "I thought he was picked up during the raid. But you stole him." He exhaled, switching to Spanish. "I want him back."

"You stole him first," said Christina, speaking French.

"I got him fair and square," he said.

"No, you didn't."

"Yes, I did."

"You snatched him out from underneath my nose," she said. "My people were already in place at the courthouse and you knew it. How is that fair?"

Pause. "Okay, you got me," he said.

"You're such a snake."

Silence.

"What now?" asked Andres.

"How should I know?" Christina moved up the stairs. "When I visited Roger in the prison hospital, he said you had the laptop."

"Roger is a liar."

"That's not new news."

"I guess you would know."

"Stay out of my personal affairs," said Christina.

"Now that you have Roger where you want him, what do you plan to do with him?"

She reached the top of the stairs and walked into her residence. She glanced at the former Deputy Attorney General. He was blindfolded and tied spread eagle to her mahogany poster bed. "I don't know yet."

THE UNCOMMITTED

CHAPTER 9

Sidney had watched her friend's eyes trail Andres out of the office. Damian Stagel gazed out of the glass-enclosed office. He watched hundreds of workers producing heroin and cocaine. He bit the inside of his lip. Sidney knew what he was thinking. They had discussed it many times. He was deeply ashamed of his past. Not only had he become involved in the horrific trade, but he had also been very successful at it. He was a wealthy man. However, in the process, he had lost his family and his real friends.

Eighteen, and grasping a prison payphone, Damian had mourned the loss of his living parents. With tears streaming down his face, he had considered suicide. The first few nights he had slept only an hour or two at a time in his cell. He had slept with his back to the wall. He had listened to the voices in the darkness. He still had nightmares. Scared and defenseless, he turned to a ring of drug dealers in jail. In exchange for their protection, he ran their underground market in prison. He was smart. He was organized. And he was among losers.

Damian had an excellent memory, committing license plate numbers, gun registration codes, and endless nicknames to memory without notes. He made himself invaluable and eventually built his own syndication. He had become what he had been wrongfully accused of by the police. Released after five years, he interviewed for legitimate jobs. Although he had earned his GED and college degree in prison, it made little difference. No one wanted to hire an ex-con. They saw a crime, not a man. He returned to the drug world. He had become a rich man destroying other people's lives.

During a trip to New Jersey, Damian had parked near his parents' home. Working up his courage, he had sat in his car looking at the small beige brick house. Just as he opened the car door and decided to ring the doorbell, he ran into a former high school basketball buddy. The friend's once trim body was now bloated, his face aged beyond his years, his hair long and unkempt. He was also grimy, disgusting, glassy-eyed and hooked on heroin. In that instant, Damian made two decisions. One, it wasn't the time to see his family yet. And two, it was time to get out of the business. His friends were either hooked on drugs or imprisoned for a quarter or more of their lives due to new mandatory federal sentences. Within months, he had laundered the drug money into legitimate businesses. He opened several automobile dealerships and collected Mexican and Italian rare coins and artifacts. He was now legitimate. The drug life was behind him.

Now this, thought Sidney. She wanted to reach out and hug him. Instead, she decided to distract him. "Wendy, check your phone," whispered Sidney. She had been right. Damian's eyes lit up. Sidney glanced out of the glass-enclosed office. The guards were focused on something else. She checked the wall camera. Was anyone watching them? Where had Andres gone so suddenly?

Shannon reached in her pocket and pulled out a cell phone. They all exhaled.

Looking expectant, Wendy Shannon placed the phone to her ear. Her face dropped. "No dial tone."

"Did you charge it?" asked Damian.

"Of course." Shannon averted her eyes. "Perhaps, we're just out of range." She glanced at the flashing red light and thought about Charles Thomas. Of course, he had been right again. Damn that man.

"Out of range?" asked Damian. "I thought it was a satellite phone. It should—"

"Well, it doesn't," snapped Shannon.

"Okay," said Sidney, holding up a hand. "Hang on to it. Maybe it'll be useful later."

Disappointed silence.

"Do you think she was serious?" asked Damian.

"Who?" asked Sidney.

"Danielle," he said. "She said it was time for her to move on."

"Oh," said Sidney.

"Crap," said Damian. He put his elbows on his thighs and rested his chin in his hand.

"Well," said Shannon, "your dead body should move that process right along,"

"Did anybody ask you?" asked Damian. "Let's see a show of hands?"

"Well, I was just saying—" started Shannon.

"Did you skip charm school altogether?" asked Damian.

"Don't get mad at me," said Shannon. "Danielle was the one who took an oath to protect the United States from criminals. And you are a criminal."

"You make me—" said Damian.

Sidney leaned forward. "More problems we do not need."

Silence filled the room.

"Drug dealer," muttered Shannon.

"Lawyer," muttered Damian.

They turned away, but cut their eyes at the other.

"Ouch," said Sidney.

"Sorry," said Damian.

Silence.

"You know, Damian," said Sidney, "I talked to Danielle right before I was . . . expelled from my life . . . and she didn't say anything to me. She confirmed the Spanish term that Charles overheard from the paramedics." Sidney thought. "Maybe she's tired from all the traveling she's been doing." Sidney bit her lip. "But now that I think about it, she did sound rather . . . irritated." She peeked at Damian and then shut her mouth.

Hunching his shoulders, Damian sighed.

Then Sidney sighed. "Michael's ex-wife is moving back to D.C.," she said.

"When?" asked Damian.

"As we speak," said Sidney. "As we speak in the heroin factory."

"Oh," said Damian.

"Crap," said Sidney.

Shannon sighed. "Charles said he met someone new."

"Charles who?" asked Damian. "I thought you collected men like dish rags."

"Something about a pot and a kettle come to mind," Shannon said, glaring at Damian.

"Charles who?" asked Sidney, looking curious.

Shannon looked from Sidney to Damian. She frowned and crossed her arms.

"Like we're going to tell anybody," said Damian.

"He does have a point," says Sidney.

Shannon dropped her arms. "Fine. Charles Thomas."

In union, Sidney and Damian said, "What!"

"Do you think he really met—" started Shannon.

"But he's so . . . decent," said Sidney, looking puzzled.

"Yeah," said Damian, "he's really decent." He looked equally perplexed.

"He said—" started Shannon again.

"Sidney, remember that day when my Jaguar stalled on Pennsylvania Avenue?" said Damian. "It had to be ninety degrees in July. He helped me push it into the Justice Department's parking lot."

"Yeah, I remember that," said Sidney. "And remember that day I had to bring in all those boxes? He stopped and helped me haul all those CSC boxes up to my office."

"Then," said Damian, scrunching up his face, "why—"

"Hey, guys," said Shannon, "Getting offended over here."

"I know, but he's—" said Sidney.

"All right, already," said Shannon. "He's too nice for the terrible Wendy. I get the general theme. Can we move off this point now?"

Both Sidney and Damian said, "But—"

Andres Santos walked into the room. He sat behind his desk and looked at the three. "How do you all feel?"

"Kidnapped," said Sidney.

"Drugged," said Damian.

"Generally pissed off," said Shannon.

"And you?" asked Sidney.

"Choosing between life, liberty and the pursuit of happiness," said Andres. He relaxed against the back of the chair. "The guards said you were quite animated in here," he said. "Where you hatching an escape plan?"

The three looked at each other.

"We were discussing your family," said Shannon. "Your sister. And your children."

"What about my sister?"

"Well, frankly, why you didn't just send her to nursing school?" asked Shannon.

"I'm training her," said Andres. "She'll be the first female drug lord in Colombia."

"Somehow, I don't think that's what Betty Friedan had in mind," said Shannon.

Andres placed his forearms on his desk. "What about my children?" he asked, interested.

"We were wondering," said Shannon, "at what age, would you start injecting heroin into their little veins?"

"What is your problem?" asked Andres. "You think it's easy being a drug lord down here? I have all sorts of pressures." He leaned back, regarding her. "There are seventeen thousand left-wing guerrillas. There are fifteen thousand right-wing paramilitary soldiers. They're trying to take over the drug trade. They're kidnapping wealthy people. They're assassinating political leaders. They're car-bombing churches. The left-wing folks are holding hostage a presidential candidate, five members of congress, eleven state legislators and a provincial governor. The right-wing folks claim to have elected dozens of candidates in the last congressional elections, and killed a few they didn't like. And all these folks want us to pay them. The government. The judges. The police. Meanwhile, we've been at war for the last forty years. The economy sucks. The churches are under siege. And we're having a class war."

"Really?" asked Shannon, looking uninterested.

Andres frowned. "Yes, in any country, war benefits somebody," said Andres. "This war happens to permit narco-trafficking, sale of weapons and huge commissions," said Andres. "Thus, the military has an interest. The elite have an interest. The guerrillas have an interest. Everybody is making money, why shouldn't I?"

"And when your daughters are blown up by a car bomb, what then?" asked Sidney.

"I do more good than most," said Andres. "I've built roads in rural villages, equipped poor schools—"

"Well, hail to Mother Teresa," said Shannon.

"Why are you so evil?" asked Andres.

———

Sitting alone in the conference room, Thomas reviewed his investigation notes. First, there was no sign of Roger Alexander. Second, Thomas had ordered military jets to sweep the Colombian countryside, searching for the three hostages. He had brushed aside complaints that the terrain was inhospitable with sheer slopes, high altitudes and few landing sites. They had covered a 350-mile spread. Thomas would not rest until they found his three friends.

Third, under his direction, the FBI had questioned the staff of Christina Savant. Did they know anything about the missing hostages or the missing felon? They did not. The agents had also questioned them about Christina's whereabouts. Unfortunately, they had corroborated her alibi. As far they knew, she had been in her office behind closed doors.

Her alibi had checked out. Her phone records had checked out. Her aircraft fleet had checked out—with each plane present and accounted for. FBI agents had then checked the passport office, commercial airlines, and flights plans for private aircrafts. Apparently, Christina Savant had not traveled to Colombia within the past week. Nor had she been in the District on the night of the kidnappings. Furthermore, neither Bruce Lewis nor Ana Santos was talking.

Nevertheless, Thomas had his agents checking every single small, privately owned plane in the United States. He didn't care that there were two hundred thousand of them. If Christina Savant had flown to Colombia this week, he intended to find out.

Sitting in his office, Andres studied Wendy Shannon. "So, you're a nicotine addict?" asked Andres.

"I'm not an addict," said Shannon.

"According to my men, when they picked you up, you were rifling through the glove compartment for a whole carton of cigarettes."

"They're legal." Shannon looked pointedly at the heroin factory.

"A cigarette is merely a highly efficient, delivery device for nicotine," said Andres. "Nicotine is as addictive as heroin or cocaine."

"You're just trying to make yourself feel better," said Shannon.

"No, actually, I wish I had come up with the idea." Andres leaned forward. "Nicotine is addictive because it triggers the release of dopamine, a chemical in the brain that's associated with feelings of pleasure."

"I'm not addicted."

"Do you need greater amounts of the drug to achieve the same level of satisfaction? Are you self-medicated to ward off withdrawal symptoms? Do you light up within five minutes of waking up? Can you go a whole day without smoking?"

"I can quit whenever I want to," said Shannon.

Andres leaned back. "All addicts say that," said Andres. "About forty percent of smokers who've had their voice boxes surgically removed . . . start smoking again. About fifty percent of smokers with lung cancer . . . start smoking again."

Shannon thought about her mother. She was still asking for a cigarette on her deathbed. "I suspect," said Shannon, "that nicotine is a lot less deadly than the animal sedative you shot us up with."

Both Damian and Sidney turned.

"That will pass out of your system within twenty-four hours," said Andres. "But the tar in your lungs won't." He stood up. "Excuse me." He walked out the door. Within ten minutes, he returned.

He stood behind Shannon's chair. "Take off your jacket."
Shannon stared over her shoulder. "I thought you said—"
"Just do as I say."
Shannon looked helplessly at Damian.
Looking very concerned, Damian stood up. "Look, man—"
Rifles cocked outside the glass walls. Hesitating, Damian glanced at Shannon.
"Just do it," said Andres. He watched as Shannon slowly removed her jacket. "Unbutton your shirt," he said.
Shannon's eyes flew around the room. "But you said—"
"Do you ever stop talking?"
She unbuttoned the top two buttons.
"Stop right there," he said. He slapped her hard on the back.
"What the hell!" cried Shannon.
"A nicotine patch," he said.
As Damian sat down with a grin, Shannon reached over her shoulder. Lo and behold, she felt a patch on her shoulder. She yanked on her blouse and jacket. She glared at him. "You could have said what you were doing," she said.
"Would you have believed me?"
She paused. "That hardly seems the point."
"Has anyone ever told you that you have anger issues?" asked Andres, raising his dark eyebrows.

———

Christina Savant straddled Roger Alexander on the bed. His wrists and ankles were tied to her mahogany bedposts. His orange prison jumpsuit had green grass stains and brownish-black burn marks. As she leaned close to his face, her red hair fell forward, brushing his cheek. She raised the blindfold from his good eye.
"Hello, my lovely," smiled Christina. "Looks like your plan blew up in your face. Literally."
"You're so witty," said Alexander.
She gazed at him in silence. His lip was a bit swollen, his scarred face scratched.

"You're just pissed because I dumped you," he said.

"There is that," she said. "And the bullet hole in my brother's chest."

"You hated him."

"So it's okay for you to shoot him?"

"He was an ass."

"Still."

"An eye for an eye, I always say," said Alexander.

She stared into his single eye. "You sure about that?"

He shifted under her, pulling at the sheets tying his wrists to the bedpost. The sheets tightened. "What do you want?" asked Alexander, frowning.

"You dead."

He paused. "What's your second choice?"

She gazed down at her former lover and former CSC colleague. He had become the former immediately after her brother had recommended him for the Deputy Attorney General post. "The missing laptop," she said.

"Bet you'd like to have those records before that grand jury hearing?" asked Alexander. "Is that still on for Monday?"

"As you're already on death row, I don't see how that concerns you," said Christina.

"I do have some thoughts about the computer."

"Well?"

"I saw you in the courtroom that day," said Alexander.

She narrowed her eyes, staring at him in silence.

Alexander blinked first. "Maybe Andres Santos has the laptop," said Alexander, looking away.

"If you were on video, I'd be fast-forwarding right now."

"Andres must—"

"He said you were lying."

"And you believe that drug dealer?" asked Alexander.

"No, I believe the one-eyed convicted felon."

Alexander exhaled deeply and shut his eye. When he opened it, he was looking up into an old French derringer. Alexander stiffened against the bed. Adrenaline rushed through his body. He was awash in a déjà vu. Four months ago, her brother's eyes had blazed when he had pulled the same pistol out of his desk drawer and pointed it at Alexander.

"I didn't expect you to kill me," said Alexander, eyebrows gathered.

"So this is a surprise?" asked Christina Savant. She tightened her thighs around his midsection.

"Yes."

"And you don't like surprises?"

"As a rule, no."

As Christina Savant stared down at him, she could not believe she had given her heart to this asshole. He had never been kind to her. After two years of some-kind-of-a-messed-up affair, she had sat in the courtroom, listening to his secretary, some married-brunette-basket-case, testify about their illicit sexual liaison. What an asshole. She should just shoot him now and be done with it.

A phone rang. She frowned at the relieved look on Alexander's face. Reluctantly, she lowered the pistol and dismounted. Keeping an eye on him, she whipped a new cell phone, with a secure line, out of her black purse. She answered, listened, frowned, smiled, and then hung up.

Swinging a taut leg over Alexander, she said, "Now, where were we? Oh, yes, now I remember." She pointed the pistol at his head.

"If you shoot me," said Alexander, "I'll have a hard time telling you where your records are."

Christine cocked her head and glanced away, her green eyes settling mid-distance. She looked down at Alexander. "Perhaps, we can reach a compromise," she said.

"Shooting me is off the table."

———

Still seated in his office, Sidney watched Andres cross his legs, ankle over knee.

"This has been entertaining," he said. "But we have drifted off the point," he said. His dark eyes narrowed. "Who has my sister? You or Christina Savant?"

The hostages were silent.

"If I don't get the right answer right now," said Andres, "we're going to have a little problem in here—"

Whiz . . . Boom! After a piercing whistling sound, there was a deafening blast outside the building. Inside, there was a splash of white light, blue electrical bursts and crackles from the office equipment. Debris fell from the ceiling; glass shattered and sprayed everywhere. Everyone dove to the floor.

"Damn," said Andres, scrambling to the floor. "This is the second factory destroyed this week. Damn. Damn. Damn. This is getting to be a habit."

Sidney crawled across the office and peered out through the glass walls. People were running everywhere. She spotted a grenade launcher. There was a loud crack overhead. She looked up. "Oh, no!" The building began to collapse around them. They scrambled amid the dust and smoke. Somewhere in the gray haze, a cell phone rang. She wasn't sure, but she thought she heard Andres saying that now was not a good time. She scampered away from his voice, toward the door. She ran smack into Damian. "Where's Wendy?" whispered Sidney. Her eyes burned from the smoke. Her nostrils filled with acidic fumes. She began coughing. She glimpsed a gray jacket. Damian reached out and grabbed a woman's arm. Who was shooting at them? Did they know they were there? Did they care?

A second blast rocked the building.

THE RANSOM RAN

CHAPTER 10

L ate Friday night. Five minutes ago. "We should meet."
Thomas pressed the phone to his ear. "I don't care if it's a bad time." He listened. "How did I get this number?" he repeated. "We are the FBI."

Saturday morning. November 1. In the cool sunshine, three security teams drove thirty miles outside the District of Columbia. Each team approached a rusty, abandoned blue tin warehouse in an open field in Virginia from three roads. They entered the warehouse from three different entrances. Inside, they set up a single pinewood table and three chairs. Eyeing each other suspiciously, each security detail swept the warehouse with hand-held bug detectors. In dark suits, with white wires in their ears, they set up surveillance receivers to hunt for other hidden transmitter devices. A light bar display would signal the presence of radio transmitters. They set up compact units to jam listening devices. They set up voice encryption systems to scramble conversations. They set up ground seismic systems, a military-style detection system, to protect the wide open space surrounding the warehouse. A remote sensor would alert them to any suspicious activity. They searched for periscopes; video cameras; wireless microphones systems; night vision capabilities; vehicle tracking systems; complete communication systems; audio patching systems for recording. They detected for concealed weapons and explosives.

Outside, they assessed all ingresses and egresses and scoped for sharpshooters. They checked the warehouse, each other's vehicles, and each other's bodies.

Saturday afternoon. Under a cloudless sky, three caravans of black shiny vans, sedans and limousines advanced from three different directions. Each moved slowly and cautiously up three white paved roads toward an abandoned blue tin warehouse. Each was armored and bullet-proof with remote bomb scanners, sirens, tear gas deterrent systems, and smoke screen systems. As they approached the warehouse, the three security teams exited the building from three entrances. They stood guard, armed to the teeth.

Each caravan stopped at a separate entrance. One person stepped into the cool sunshine from each convoy and entered the warehouse. Each sat at the pinewood table.

"Afraid that I might shoot you?" asked Charles Thomas, staring across the table.

"Being prepared is being prepared without notice," said Christina Savant.

"I think I speak for everyone here," said Andres Santos, "when I say that no one wants a tape of this meeting showing up on the evening news."

"Let's discuss a prisoner exchange," said Thomas, without expression. "Who has who?"

The dark eyes and the emerald eyes across from him offered nothing.

"Fine. I'll start," said Thomas. "Ana Santos is in federal custody. Charged with enough federal offenses that neither of you will ever see her again."

The dark eyes shifted. The green eyes remained impassive.

"And?" said Christina.

"And," said Thomas, "we located the owner of the eight-seater jet you charted to Colombia. We've taken his deposition and his deposit slip for the ten thousand dollars in cash you paid him. He's identified your photo and is eager to point you out in a line-up. Turns out he's in his late fifties with two kids in college and doesn't want to lose his pilot license or go to jail. I empathize." He paused. "And your grand jury hearing is still on for Monday."

Silence.

"So," said Thomas, "which one of you has Roger Alexander now?"

"She does," said Andres, nodding his head.

Thomas looked at Andres. "This was after you shot Alexander with the animal tranquilizer we found on the cot in your factory?" Thomas watched a dark eyebrow rise.

"Have you no shame?" asked Christina, cutting her eyes at Andres.

"What?" asked Andres. "You must be kidding?"

"Do you have Roger Alexander?" asked Thomas, studying Christina.

"What do you have that I want?" asked Christina.

"Your freedom," said Thomas.

Silence.

"Who has Sidney, Damian and Wendy?" asked Thomas. He leaned forward.

"That depends on who tried to blow me up," said Andres.

"When?" asked Thomas.

"Last night," said Andres.

"Then I'm out," said Thomas, throwing up his hands and leaning back.

Andres glared at Christina. He watched her shrug her slender shoulders. "Remind me to splash you with some holy water," said Andres. "What is up with women these days?" He shook his head and then focused on Thomas. "In that case, I do," said Andres. "I have Sidney and Damian."

"What about Wendy?" asked Thomas. His forehead was wrinkled, anxious.

"Her, too," said Andres, sounding exasperated. His expression relaxed. "So you're that Charles Thomas?" He leaned back in chair, wearing a grin. "Wendy's spoken of you."

"What did she say?" asked Thomas.

Andres stared at the Deputy Director of the United States Federal Bureau of Investigation. "What do you mean what did she say?" asked Andres. "What are you thinking, man?"

Thomas tried to suppress a smile. "I know," said Thomas. "I can't help myself."

Three cell phones rang. They patted suit pockets or checked a purse. Each pulled out a phone and glanced at the incoming telephone number. Eyebrows rose. Each said, "Excuse me." Chairs scrapped the floor as they stood and hustled out the three exits. Overhead, gray clouds were darkening. Within seconds, doors were slamming; engines racing.

THE TRIPLE CROSS

CHAPTER 11

Saturday evening. As darkness fell, Sidney stepped out of the dense forest and the thick underbrush into a clear landing. She noticed that the virgin forest had been cut and cleared. Sweet scents glided in the air. Her brown eyes passed over a panoramic view of the Blue Ridge Mountains. Wildflowers grew along the fertile banks of a tranquil lake. A large dock, boathouse, and deck gradually sloped into the placid lake. She stepped forward. In the center of a mountain cove sat a large cottage. Pulling a .357 Magnum from her waistband, Sidney moved toward the cottage.

Sidney had acquired the gun from the cousin of Andres Santos. As his factory was collapsing after the blast, the bandaged man had slammed into Wendy, trying to get to Andres. They had gone down in the rubble. He had managed to break Wendy's arm and get himself kidnapped in the process. Damian had grabbed him on the way out of the door. Cornered like a trapped rat, he had proven quite useful in getting them out of the rain forest, back to civilization, to a doctor, and on a plane heading out of Colombia.

Cautiously, Sidney now circled the retreat, gripping the gun. In the rear, there were several large windows, including two bay windows. She imaged a breathtaking view of beautiful woods and mountains on a clear day. Facing a window, she pushed it. She pushed harder. It didn't budge. Despite the twinge in her back, she tried another window. No luck. She tried a third. It didn't budge. She stepped back and reassessed. The bay windows were above her head. She would have to try the front, she thought. She took two steps, passing the back door. She stepped back two steps and tried the doorknob. The door opened. Her eyebrows flew up. Her heart beat a little faster. Her eyes darted around the large backyard. She didn't see anyone. She looked up to the darkening sky. She heard thunder in the distance. Clouds drifted over a full moon.

Sidney opened the door warily, stepping inside. Her eyes narrowed, focusing in the darkness of the large house. She passed through a recreational room. In the shadows, she saw the outlines of a pool table, cue sticks hanging on a nearby wall and chairs scattered about. She bumped into one. She clinched her teeth. Why was she always bumping into furniture? She moved past the play room, through a large eat-in kitchen, and made her way down a dark narrow hallway. Old-fashioned pictures hung on the walls. She treaded lightly on the hardwood floor. She passed two bedrooms, a bathroom, and a staircase leading upstairs. She heard the soft crackle of wood burning in a fireplace. There was a scent of burning virgin wood.

As she neared the end of the corridor, Sidney raised the pistol. She hesitated. She stepped into a dimly lit living room. Her eyes quickly scanned the large room. It was filled with dark wood furniture, and dark green and maroon rugs covered the hardwood floors.

"I thought you might come."

Sidney spun toward the voice, bracing the gun in front of her. Something moved in the shadows behind her. Confused, she turned.

Moving quickly, Roger Alexander pressed a gun in her ribcage. He wrenched the gun out of her hand. Smiling, he backed away from her. He was bathed in the light from the fireplace. "I have to give you your due. You are smart."

"The laptop is here?" asked Sidney.

Alexander nodded. The small gray computer, with a blue CSC logo, sat on a large desk. A screwdriver lay next to it. Nearby was a small gray metal box with a green computer chip.

"Is that the hard drive?" asked Sidney.

Alexander walked to the desk, picked it up and tossed it into the fireplace. The odor of plastic and metal burning drifted into the room. The hard drive melted and blistered. Small bursts and crackles filled the room.

"The big bad is back," said Alexander, turning with a smug expression.

Something moved in the shadows again. "Hello, my lovely." There was a loud sizzle and a crackle.

Alexander screamed as he fell to the floor. The French derringer and the .357 Magnum slid across the floor.

Backing up, Sidney's eyes flew to the door.

"What a load of crap," said Christina Savant, stepping out of the shadows in a cobalt suit.

"Shit!" Alexander withered on the floor, grabbing his burning behind. "You're really starting to get on my nerves." He stared up at the black stun gun. The smell of burning flesh filled the room.

With cobalt high heels, Christina kicked the guns across the floor, away from Alexander. "Well, you should give that some thought the next time you plan an escape." She frowned. "Here I am in the middle of high-level negotiations and it turns out that the ransom ran."

Silence and glares all around.

"Maybe we can work together," said Alexander.

"Has the voltage affected your mind?" asked Christina.

Sidney suppressed a chuckle.

"So you discovered the back exit out of Savant Plaza?" asked Christina.

"It helped that you hadn't shared that little factoid with your people," said Alexander.

They glowered at each other.

Christina scanned the room. Her eyes stopped at the desk. "CSC laptop?"

Roger Alexander simply stared at her.

Christina stepped closer to him, wrapping a manicured finger around the trigger of the stun gun.

"Yes," he said.

She gazed at it. Her eyes moved to the dying fire. She listened to the popping embers. "The hard drive?"

"Yes," said Alexander, single eye glued to the gun.

"Well done," she said, appearing self-satisfied.

Keeping her eyes on him, she crossed the floor. She picked up the derringer. "A family heirloom," she said, dropping it into her leather purse. "Just in case." She dropped Sidney's .357 Magnum in her purse as well.

Standing slightly behind Christina, Sidney moved toward the door.

Christina turned toward her, flinging her red hair over her shoulder. "How did you know to come here?"

Sidney stopped moving. "What? Oh, uh . . . it's a great place for a celebrity felon to hide," said Sidney. "And the owner is dead, thus, it's probably empty. Might even have food supplies. In Virginia, not too far from the District." She did not mention the other reason she had thought to look here. Instead, it just showed up.

"Yes, the owner is dead," repeated Christina. Her eyes hardened. Thinking about her brother, she stepped closer to Alexander. Her finger eased around the trigger.

Alexander flinched, squeezing his eye shut.

Nothing. No sizzle. No crackle. No nothing. He opened his eye.

Sidney looked around.

Andres Santos was standing there. He was pointing a .38 pistol at Christina's head.

"Hello, Christina," said Andres.

She whirled around. "You're like everywhere," sighed Christina "How did you know we were here?"

Andres looked around. "Laptop?" he asked. Roger pointed at the desk. "Hard drive?" Roger pointed at the fireplace. The last cinders of the fire were dying in the fireplace.

Sidney moved toward the door again.

Andres whirled around to scan each face in the room. "Roger, did you send out invitations?" He looked at Alexander. "How did everyone know to come here?" The room was barely illuminated by moonlight; passing clouds eclipsed the pale light. "First, somebody turn on a light, I can't see a damn thing in here."

Standing next to the door, behind a chair, Sidney flicked on the overhead light. "Let's see a show of hands," said Sidney. "How many people here got calls from Bruce Lewis?"

Every hand in the room went up.

"Okay, I'm impressed," said Andres. "He's got cojones."

"Yeah," said Alexander, "and I'm going to hook 'em up to electrodes the next time I see him."

Silent nods.

"Well, instead of killing each other, as expected," said Alexander, raising himself onto one elbow, "we could actually work together."

"Either that," said Andres, "or I could shoot you all right now." He turned, taking the stun gun from Christina. He dropped it into the pocket of his black suit jacket. "Hmm, let's see. What to do? What to d—"

Crack!

Sidney had picked up a chair and bashed him over the head. He smashed to the floor. His .38 pistol clattered to the floor. It slid across the hardwood floor, spun around and stopped between Alexander and Christina. Everyone stared at it. They looked up, staring at each other.

Alexander jumped to his feet, lunging forward. Christina reached in her purse, whipped out the old derringer, and fired. There was a loud explosion. A puff of black smoke drifted in the air. Everyone in the room stared at Alexander. He grabbed his chest. His eye swirled in confusion. He stared down at his chest. He pulled his fingers away. There was no sticky dark red blood. A grin slowly crossed his thin lips. The derringer had misfired.

"Jesus H. Christ," said everyone in the room.

"You're like the undead," said Sidney.

In a flash, Christina and Alexander were on top of each other, struggling on the floor for the .38 pistol. There was a lot of kicking, scratching and a few smacks. Mostly from Christina. Nevertheless, Alexander came up with the pistol.

They both shot to their feet.

"I should shoot you," said Alexander. His eye wandered about; apparently in shock from several blows to the head. His hand pressed against his forehead.

"Who?" asked Andres, staggering to his feet. His hand rubbed the back of his head.

"Yeah, you could be a bit more specific," said Sidney. Her hand massaged her aching back.

Christina stood with a hand on her hip, looking aggravated.

Alexander's eye settled down. Unfortunately, it settled on Sidney. He pointed the weapon at her. "I lost my job. I lost my reputation. My freedom. My damn eye," said Alexander, putting a hand to his head. "And it's all your fault."

Sidney looked baffled. "In what twisted world is this my fault?"

They stared at each other. Rain pounded the roof and splattered against the windows.

"That's a point," he said, turning the gun on Christina.

Christina pointed a finger at Andres Santos. "He shot you up with animal tranquilizer."

"What!?" said Alexander. "Have you no shame?"

"That's what I said," said Christina.

Andres cocked his head toward Christina. "She offered you up to the feds."

Alexander turned on Christina.

Christina shrugged her shoulders. "Well, you're already on death row, how much worse could it get?"

"What!?" Alexander looked from Christina to Andres. "Never mind," said Alexander. His eye passed over everyone in the room. "I can't work with you people."

Overhead, they heard the beating blades of a large helicopter. Sidney glanced out the window. A large UH-60 Black Hawk helicopter swung into view. A pair of GAU-17 Gatling machine guns were on each side. Sidney hit the light switch. They were plunged into darkness.

"Nobody move!" shouted Alexander.

Sidney heard a lot of moving. There was a blast and a flash of gunfire. Her body crashed to the floor. Sidney felt the coolness of the hardwood floor. One hand lay on the rough edges of a floor rug. She felt someone brush by her and then felt cool air rushing into the room, as a door opened and then slammed shut.

"I said—" started Alexander.

"Don't move!" shouted a voice from the doorway. It was deep and male.

The room was suddenly flooded with light. Sidney felt herself being hauled to her feet. Standing, she stared into the dark brown eyes of Charles Thomas. A squad of FBI agents rushed into the room. In black jackets with yellow lettering, they were heavily armed with rifles and small firearms. Water dripped onto the hardwood floors.

Sidney looked around. "Christina Savant is gone," said Sidney.

"Secure the house," ordered Thomas. His men immediately moved into position, pointing large assault weapons at Roger Alexander and Andres Santos. "Search the woods."

"She may be armed," said Sidney.

"Christina Savant may be armed and dangerous," shouted Thomas. "Also, search the room for weapons." He watched his men collect various weapons.

"Are you all right?" asked Thomas, looking her over.

"I'm fine," said Sidney, searching herself for bullet holes and finding none.

They watched the commotion in the room.

"You got a call from Bruce Lewis?" asked Sidney.

"Yeah, how did you know?" asked Thomas.

"Bruce was the only person with means, motive, and opportunity," said Sidney. "One, he was in the courtroom that day. With the laptop. He knew what was on it. He knew about this cottage—Peter Savant's cottage. He knew the connection between Alexander, Andres and Christina. He knew they'd destroy the evidence. And he knew that if these people were put in a room together, that someone—or everyone—would end up buried out in the backyard." She had remembered the cottage while in Andres's office. With flashing markers, his wall map had pinpointed all of Peter Savant's homes.

"So you're okay?" asked Thomas, looking her over again.

From his anxious expression, Sidney assumed he was searching for bullet holes. "No one was shot," she said.

His face relaxed.

"Did you pick up Damian and Wendy?" asked Sidney.

"I had a unit of agents pick them up." Worry edged his voice. "Wendy is on her way to the hospital. They tell me she needs to have her arm set, but otherwise she's fine."

Sidney smiled at him knowingly. "Good."

He blushed.

Andres stepped forward. Agents cocked rifles. He put his hands up. "If your winner-takes-all deal is still on the table, I'm your guy."

"Don't need a guy," said Thomas. "Already got a girl."

"Who?" asked Alexander and Andres.

"Christina is in the wind," said Andres.

"Your sister," said Thomas.

"Ana?" asked Andres. His lipped curled in disbelief. "She'd rather die first."

"Apparently not," said Thomas.

"Damn!" said Alexander. He flung his arms up in frustration.

"Why?" asked Andres. His eyes filled with hurt. "Why would she do that?"

They stared at him. Facing his own hypocrisy, his face reddened.

"She's young and life imprisonment is a long time," said Sidney. "Execution is worse."

Shaking his head in agreement, Thomas said, "With Ana's testimony, we're interdicting, eradicating, and seizing every asset, every piece of property, and every dollar you have. Residences, vehicles, boats, aircraft, weapons, millions in cash. We're destroying the meth, the cocaine, the heroin, the ecstasy. Simultaneous raids are under way—right now—in Colombia, Brazil, Bolivia, Ecuador and St. Kitts."

THE BEGINNING

CHAPTER 12

Early Sunday morning. Staring straight ahead, Shannon ignored the fast-food places, gas stations and three-story apartment buildings lining the busy avenue. This was the third time that she had waffled on her decision since turning her dented green car onto New York Avenue. Heading into the heart of the District, she checked her rearview mirror. She glimpsed a green traffic sign. It pointed to New York City. Going in the opposite direction. That was a third option. With a U-turn, she could be in Manhattan inside of four hours. Maybe she could start over there. Perhaps, she could live a quiet life, leaving her mistakes behind. She had slept with too many men. She had accused too many innocent people. She had offended nearly everybody. She needed to live her life in moderation, not swinging from extreme to extreme.

Driving with her broken arm, set in a hard cast, but still throbbing, she reached in the glove compartment with her other hand, found a cigarette, and slipped it between her lips. Her hand rifled around in her small black purse until she felt the slick outside of a matchbook. With one hand, she opened the matchbook, extracted a match and lit it. As her hand moved toward the end of the cigarette, she thought about her mother. She had chain-smoked herself to death. At the age of 42, she had been diagnosed with stage IV lung cancer. Before she sought medical treatment, she had a cough, chest pains, and a fever. As the lung cancer spread to other organs, pain filled her bones, her skin and eyes turned yellow, and tumor masses grew near her neck. Later, it spread to her heart and her windpipe. As it worsened, her mother had rotated between anxiety, fear, and anger. As she moved toward the latter, her father had stopped Wendy's visits. Later, they had a closed casket funeral. Her father had merely said there was nothing left to see.

Before her mother's death, Shannon had copied her father's behavior. Now, she realized for the first time that he had not been cool and distant, but rather cold and unconcerned. She remembered the hurt in her mother's dark green eyes. She had watched her husband and her daughter move around the room as though they were strangers. At least twice, Shannon recalled her mother asking to see her alone. Her father had declined, whisking her out of the room.

Shannon was nearing her forty-third birthday. She exhaled and made a decision. She made several turns until she reached Michigan Avenue, a large tree-lined boulevard. Ahead, a blue mosaic dome towered over a multi-ethnic, middle-class neighborhood filled with Queen Anne-style homes, Victorian cottages and a Catholic university. She glanced up at the Basilica of the National Shrine of the Immaculate Conception. She parked in front of the lavish cathedral. What did her mother want to tell her? Would she have warned her against men like her father? Men who offered no love, no passion . . . only material things.

She took the cigarette from her lips, broke it in half, and dropped it in her ashtray. What had she read? Something about cigarette companies dumping like six hundred additives into these things—ammonia, arsenic, lead, and formaldehyde. Formaldehyde, for god's sake. What was that about? No wonder the "Marlboro Man" had dropped dead from lung cancer. She dug in her purse and found a newly purchased nicotine patch. She pulled up the sleeve of her simple navy dress and pressed the patch to her arm. She took off her round-rimmed glasses. She looked at them. They were exactly like her father's. She tossed them into the glove compartment. Peering into the rearview mirror, she popped in contact lens. She added a light touch of toasted almond lipstick to her lips. She stared at her face. She had brushed her short blonde hair until it shone. Delicate pearl earrings adorned her ears. She had a few reddish-blue bruises where her face had banged into the steering wheel during her kidnapping. Her gray eyes shifted from the rearview mirror to the cathedral. Was she doing the right thing? The palms of her hands began to sweat. She licked her lips and wiped her hands on the dress. She could still go the office. She should be preparing Ana Santos for the grand jury hearing tomorrow. She frowned. She smoothed her dress over her thick hips. "Oh, well." She wasn't perfect and she never would be; no point in letting that stop her now. She exhaled as she chose a third option for her life—different from her father and her mother.

Strolling up the main entrance, she fell in behind the other late arrivals entering the Great Upper Church. As her eyes adjusted to the darkness, they rose up the mosaic of "Christ and Majesty," the centerpiece in the Upper Church. Unsure of herself, she walked further up the aisle. Why wasn't he here? Disappointed, she turned to leave.

"Wendy?"

Shannon turned at the sound of her name. The soft smile on his lips warmed her heart.

She walked toward Charles Thomas. When she reached him, she hugged him.

"Are you all right?" he asked, looking at the cast.

"I am now," she said.

"I prayed for you."

"Really?" asked Shannon.

He reached into his pocket, took out her security badge and handed it to her.

"How long have you had that in your pocket?" asked Shannon.

"Since the night you disappeared."

Her eyes filled with tears. "Is your offer still on the table?" asked Shannon, getting chocked up on the last word. "That you want to love me?"

"Yes."

"I'd like that," said Wendy.

Sunday afternoon. Exhausted, Damian Stagel entered his Dupont Townhouse. He had spent part of the night at the hospital with Wendy Shannon. The medical treatment for her arm had been complicated by the animal sedative flowing in her veins. When he was sure that she had been safely treated, he drove her home and put her to bed. As aggravating as she was, she had grown on him, sort of like fungi. He had then driven ninety-miles an hour to New Jersey. In the middle of the night, he had confronted his parents. They had two choices—to accept him as is or to watch him walk away. They could call when they were ready. He had then showered, changed and driven ninety-miles an hour back to the District. He had made one more stop and now, he was here.

Unlike the last time he was home, there was no crackling fire. No wonderful spices scenting the air. No wine chilling. His elbows and knees still throbbed from crashing into the motorcycle and landing in the street. He took a deep breath. Was that a whiff of her perfume? He pursued the soft scent through the apartment to his back bedroom. A neat ponytail of long brownish-black hair hung down her back. She wore a pink sweat suit and white sneakers. As an inner peace washed over him, he relaxed his long body against the door jamb. She had engaged his intellect, ignoring his looks. She had accepted his life, ignoring his past. She had encouraged a relationship with his parents, ignoring his inability to commit. She was good for him and good to him.

She turned slowly, hiding something behind her back. Damian couldn't read the emotion in her dark brown eyes.

"What you got there?" asked Damian.

"Who's asking?" She sounded tentative.

"Your husband-to-be."

Her dark eyes widened. She pulled her hands from behind her back. She held them out like a small child. "Just this," she said.

Damian looked at the white shirt. It was the shirt he had worn the night he disappeared. He had taken it off before their Jacuzzi adventure.

"What are you doing with my shirt?"

"It smells like you," she said.

"Come here," said Damian.

Her face softened into a smile as she ran across the room and threw herself at him. He smiled and grabbed her legs as they wrapped around his waist. He had to catch the door to keep them from falling backwards. They were laughing and kissing.

"Hello, Danielle," said Damian.

She kissed his earlobes, his cheeks and his forehead.

"I think you missed a spot," he grinned.

She pulled back and peered at him seriously. "Where?"

"Here," he said. He scrunched up his face so that his nose stuck out.

She kissed him on the end of his nose.

"I've got something behind my back, too," said Damian, shifting her to one side. He pulled a small square box out of his back pants pocket. He flipped open the box. Her eyes never left his. If she had looked down, she would have seen a stunning three-carat, emerald-cut diamond ring.

"I had all sorts of thoughts—that you wouldn't come back," said Danielle.

"Is that a yes?" asked Damian.

"I'll never leave you."

———————

Sunday night. The reddish-orange sun was descending in the horizon as Sidney Cox drove out of the District. She turned into a familiar neighborhood and parked her car in the driveway of a two-story, tan brick home. She popped the trunk to her rental car. Her mind drifted as she walked around the car. On the drive over, after a quick stop by her parents' Georgetown house, she had received a call from Damian and Danielle. They had all screamed at the news of the impending nuptials of her best friend. Damian was truly happy for the first time since their arrest as teenagers.

They were turning their lives around. Along with the FBI Director, Sidney had made the circuit of the Sunday morning political talk shows. The kidnappings had added urgency to

President Wright's announcement. Tomorrow morning, she would stand with him as he announced his South American Marshal Plan—a multi-billion-dollar package. It was a real war on drugs. Aerial surveillance and crop destruction would wipe out cocoa and poppy crops. Alternative crop production would increase rural jobs with decent wages. Drug treatment would save addicts and empty the jails of small-time users. They now had the money and the mandate. They would use the DEA, the FBI, the Pentagon, the Coast Guard, the Army, and the United States Treasury. Midterm elections were on Tuesday and the President's party would take control of both the U.S. House and the Senate. They were on the verge of something great.

As Sidney reached into the trunk of her car, she smiled. All the promotions that had been announced in July were assured. Paul Martinez, Charles Thomas, and the FBI Director would move up to FBI Deputy Director, FBI Director and Attorney General, respectively. They had worked hard and had made a difference. The Vice President and his wife, who had pushed for Alexander's appointment to the Justice Department, had taken some hits, but had survived. Moreover, Sidney and Thomas had convinced the President to keep Wendy Shannon on board. He had been livid over her television debacle with Alexander's mother. Thinking about Wendy Shannon made Sidney want to whistle "If I Only Had a Brain" from the *Wizard of Oz*. Yet, there was something about her. Sidney couldn't quite put her finger on it. Anyway, Sidney assumed that Shannon was in the office right now, preparing for the grand jury hearing in the morning. However, if she had any sense at all, she would be somewhere snuggling with that fine Charles Thomas. Sidney shook her head. Love was a mystery. Or perhaps, she had underestimated Ms. Shannon.

Sidney cocked her head as she pulled two large pieces of black luggage from her trunk. She grimaced. Her back still ached from the elevator calamity. Stretching her back, Sidney set the luggage on the driveway and shut the trunk. Sidney had once watched the Attorney General and envied his life. He had had a great wife, family, home, and career. However, his life had been cut short, a casualty in a war that had not yet begun. She would learn from his life. She would also learn from the life of Bruce Lewis. Here was a man who had made all the wrong choices, but in the end, he had fought to protect his wife and two young sons. Apparently, a skinny prison guard had given him access to a phone when told that the purpose was to stick it to Roger Alexander. When Alexander was told about the guard, he was heard muttering something like, "Should have killed that little pissant when I had the chance." *Retribution could be swift and merciless*, thought Sidney.

Lugging the heavy luggage, Sidney walked to the front door, rang the doorbell and thought about her next steps. Now, all they had to do was decide who got the reward. There was a twenty-five-million-dollar reward on the head of Andres Santos and Roger Alexander, each. There would probably be a bigger reward for the capture of Christina Savant. She was still at large. And there was that missing bullet. Someone had fired a gun; however, no bullet was ever found. Well, that was not her problem. Today, Sidney had bigger catfish to fry. A big smile crossed her lips. She was finally home. She had found her place in life. She waited. The door opened slowly. Her smile widened.

Sidney blinked twice. A striking woman stood in the doorway. Her skin was smooth cocoa brown; her make-up flawless; her shiny black hair pinned up, with tendrils falling softly about her oval face. Sidney opened her mouth and then closed it. She stepped back from the door. "I'm sorry . . . I must . . ." She looked up and down the street. Her eyes paused on an olive Lexus, with a banged-up bumper, parked nearby. She glanced at the black numbers next to the door. She had the right house. Her mind was a blank.

"You're at the right house," said the other woman, smoothly. "I'm Michael Hollander's *wife*."

Sidney blinked rapidly.

"You must be Sidney," she said, holding the door. "We've been reading all about you in the newspapers. Michael and I have been so sorry to hear about your . . . accident. We—"

"Oh, you're Michael's *ex-wife*" said Sidney, collecting herself. "Are the kids visiting?"

"No."

The two women gazed at each other.

"This is not my happy ending, is it?" asked Sidney. The other woman was silent. Sidney exhaled and set her bags down.

Michael appeared behind the other woman. His eyes absorbed the scene. Sidney wore black boots, snug hip-hugger jeans and a white blouse. Her hair was brushed back from her pretty face; her brown eyes apprehensive; her dimples absent. Two large suitcases sat at her feet. "Yes, it is," he said. He stepped out, picked up the bags, glanced down at his ex-wife, and carried the luggage into the house and up the stairs.

Sidney couldn't help it, but a big grin crossed her face. Dimples emerged.

"This isn't over," whispered the other woman.

Sidney simply grinned.

Michael returned and said, "Thanks for stopping by, Vanessa." He locked eyes with his ex-spouse. His face was firm, his stance clear.

"If that's the way you want it, Michael," said his ex-wife, scowling with her hands on her hips.

"That's the way it is," said Michael.

She glared at Sidney. After two beats, she stalked out the door. Michael watched her leave and then turned his full attention to Sidney.

"Welcome home, sweetness," smiled Michael.

Sidney stepped inside and gave him a big hug and kiss. Then she closed the door to her new home.

The Happy Ending.

Let my enemies devour each other.

—Salvador Dali

Excerpts

Act of Vengeance & Abuse of Power

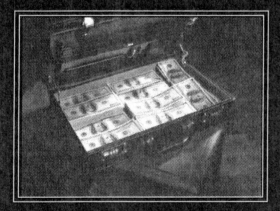

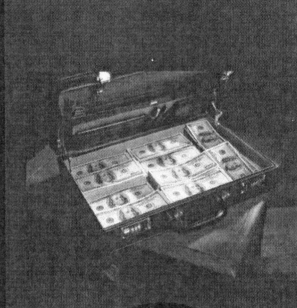

A Thriller Series

ACT OF VENGEANCE

by

Millicent Y. Hodge, Esq.

PROLOGUE

DECEMBER

THE LIST

Mr. Roger Alexander

Mr. Charles Thomas

Mr. Richard Spaulding

Mr. Mark Hastings

OUTSIDE

WASHINGTON, D.C.

ROGER ALEXANDER

"Your appeal was rejected."
"I do not intend to die on death row."
"Where do you intend to die?"
"I don't."

The two men stared at each other in silence. The inmate's dark right eye was steady; his left eye sutured shut. Although his index finger leisurely traced the deep, pinkish-red scars on his face, his bulky, six-two frame was poised for battle.

"If you want a miracle, you should call a priest," said the lawyer.

The inmate blinked slowly. In the distance, a jingle of keys echoed in the maximum security unit.

Tall, trim and courtly with silver hair, the lawyer averted his gaze. His eyes fixed on the black stamp on his client's orange jumpsuit—Lynnwood Correctional Facility. Roger Alexander had once been a very powerful man.

"Where's the new FBI Director?" asked Alexander. "I'm surprised that he isn't here to give me the news himself."

"He's on a plane."

Silence.

"What's the next step?" asked Alexander.

A partner in a silk-stocking law firm, the lawyer exhaled and leaned against the dense metal door of the ten-by-twelve cell. "Against my better judgment, we appealed this case to the D.C. Court of Appeals. It normally takes sixty-eight days from argument to termination. The court decided your case in four days. They're sending you a message."

"Can we petition for a rehearing?"

"The court entered a judgment on Christmas Eve. The court never works on Christmas Eve."

"An en banc rehearing?" asked Alexander.

"You want to go before the same court, just with more judges?"

"Why not?"

"Those petitions are rarely granted."

"Another appeal then?"

"You want to take this case before the Supreme Court?" asked the lawyer. "You shot a man – with a very nice pearl handle pistol – in open court. You escaped from federal custody – after you were convicted. And while you were out and about, you did some other very nasty things – all along the way – while you were a fugitive from justice." He crossed his arms. "And you want me to take this case before the Supreme Court?"

"I did plead insanity."

"Perhaps, we should have won," said the lawyer.

Near

Nairobi, Kenya

CHARLES THOMAS

Thirty minutes later, a cab screeched to a halt and the FBI Director jumped out and sprinted through the Jomo Kenyatta International Airport. Clutching a small black suitcase, he darted through crowds of holiday travelers. Red and green Christmas lights became a blur as he ran faster. He passed a bureau de change, several restaurants, a post office and a duty free shop. Behind him, the ambassador hustled to keep up. Out of breath, the director reached the ticket counters first. His eyes scanned the thirty counters. He stepped in front of one. "Where's Air Force Two?" he panted. "I have to get on that plane." Air Force One was being used by the President.

A young ticket agent turned and stopped short. Her eyes passed over his handsome face and broad shoulders. She took in his expression and then looked down at her computer. "May I have your name?"

"Charles Thomas," he said, leaning over the green counter.

Her dark fingers flew over the keyboard. "Yes, Mr. Thomas. You were scheduled to be cleared out here on Air Force Two." She checked her watch. "Five minutes ago."

"Can he still catch it if we hurry?" asked the ambassador, arriving at the counter. His small chest heaved in and out has he struggled to catch his breath. He glanced toward the thirteen gates.

"I'm afraid not," said the attendant, pointing toward the glass front of the airport. On the runway, a plane lifted off into the crystal blue sky. Escorted by six F-16 fighter jets, it raced toward the golden glow of the sun. "That was Air Force Two."

APPROACHING

NEW YORK CITY

RICHARD SPAULDING IV

"**B**id whist anyone?" asked the Vice President. With glee, he gathered up the cards lying on table.

The double doors opened and his secretary poked her head into the stateroom of Air Force II. It was a conference-dining room filled with cherry wood furniture, warm gray and beige fabric and retractable wall maps. A muted television set was turned to CNN in a large wall cabinet. Richard Spaulding was not surprised to see the door open. Half of the twenty-six guests on board, all VIPs, moved between here and the two passenger compartments in the rear of the Boeing 707. It pissed off the Secret Service, but Spaulding didn't care. He liked having his friends around.

"Your wife is on line one, sir," said the brunette secretary.

"Thank you." Spaulding whirled around in his executive chair, picked up the line and then turned back to face the secretary. "Have you heard from Charles Thomas yet?"

"Yes, sir," she said. "He had trouble getting through, but he's arranged for an alternative flight. He'll arrive in New York shortly after us."

"Good." Spaulding glanced out of the plane's small windows. Rain drops speckled the small double-pane glass. As far as he could see, the dark Atlantic Ocean stretched out before the plane. "Maybe he'll make his friend's engagement party tonight." This trip had gotten Spaulding great press, some interesting deals and time with key Congressional members. Charles Thomas had been very helpful in putting this trip together.

"Do you need anything else, sir?" asked the secretary, smiling pleasantly.

"No." Spaulding glanced at her shapely calves as she retreated. As the double doors shut, he glimpsed the blue uniform of the pilot. Spaulding wondered if he was headed upstairs to the nerve center. A high-tech telecommunication system was on the top level of the plane. Spaulding like neither the cold austere blue and gray of the third level nor the technocrats who worked up there.

Spaulding hit the pulsing red line. "Hi, Sugar."

"Hi yourself."

"I have plans for you tonight," he whispered into the phone.

"Is that so?" she said, "because I have plans for you." Her voice was soft and halting.

He imagined her dark eyes, the shiny black hair that framed her oval face and her soft skin. He had been lured in by the small black mole at the corner of her mouth. It was seductive and wild, like her. During their lovemaking, he couldn't take his eyes off it.

He pressed the phone closer to his ear. "What kind of plans?" he asked, intrigued.

She paused. "Special plans."

He had met Victoria Saunders four years ago. She had been hired by his assistant as the photographer for his last Senatorial campaign. For six months, she had traveled on his campaign bus. Although she was tall and striking, he had paid little attention to her until one radiant Sunday morning. She had stepped on the bus wearing a short white sundress and large dark sunglasses. Her hair, always straight and pinned in a graceful chignon, was curly, untamed and flowed to her bare shoulders. She had reminded him of someone, but he couldn't place who until much later. They were engaged during President's Wright first race for the White House; just days before he selected a Vice President. Many months later, Spaulding wed her in an elaborate White House ceremony. She quickly enchanted the nation, who now knew her simply as "Sugar." When she let it slip she was expecting—the first White House pregnancy since the Kennedy's—the Spaulding were exulted to star status.

"Where are you?" asked Spaulding.

"The pilot tells me we're right behind you."

"How was your trip to Paris?"

"Great."

He heard a click on the phone line. "Did you hear that?" asked Spaulding, stiffening.

"Hear what?" she asked. "No, I didn't hear anything."

He relaxed. "How are you feeling?"

"It must have been a man who named this morning sickness. For two months, I've been sick morning, noon and night."

"It'll get better."

"That's easy for you to say," she laughed. "Hang on for a minute."

He heard her cover the mouth-piece. There were muffled voices in the background. He was distracted by the Secretary of State's gritty voice behind him. She debated with Senator Harlin about the last card game. The Vice President glanced over his shoulder. Harlin wore a smug grin and fingered his red bow tie. Spaulding's view was blocked as his assistant, Jack, walked by, heading toward the lavatory. Turning, Spaulding set his elbows on the table and his mind drifted while he waited. His new wife had already shaken thousands of hands; spoken at hundreds of fundraisers and rallies. Her poll numbers exceeded his own. So far, she was getting everything right. But what about when he ran for President? It was several years away, but it weighed heavily on his mind. How would Sugar deal with the pressure?

She had been tested when Roger Alexander was arrested for murder. The administration had been rocked. Alexander was their top guy at Justice. The media had feasted on the scandal for weeks. They zeroed in on Sugar. Friends with Alexander, she had recommended him for the Attorney General post. However, after Alexander's conviction, she had distanced herself from the scandal with calm assurance and was ignoring his plea to an appeals court. Spaulding was impressed. His new wife had dealt with the media as well as he, and he had been raised in a political family. Barring any new scandals, President Wright would be re-elected next year, serve out his second term and then the Spauldings would step up to the plate.

"This is your captain speaking."

Spaulding glanced up, listening to the intercom. The pilot was back where he belonged.

"We'll be landing at JFK International Airport momentarily." The pilot hesitated. "We're flying into a thunderstorm. So, there may be some turbulence as we head into New York. For everyone's safety, please take your seats."

Spaulding heard Sugar remove her hand from the receiver. "The new pilot," she said, "says we'll get into Kennedy Airport right behind you. If you wait, we can take the same helicopter to the fundraiser—"

"You have a new pilot?" he asked, mildly surprised. Although she had first pick of the twenty aircraft in the Presidential fleet, with the exception of Air Force One and Two, she always flew the same Boeing 747 jumbo jet with the same crew. She said it calmed her nerves.

She paused and then said, "I can see your plane." She sounded pleased.

He imagined his plane cruising at six hundred miles per hour through the dark sky between six smaller aircraft. The American Flag on the tail and the Presidential seal on its nose. Weeks into his term, he had rescued the aircraft from an Ohio museum. To get it, he had battled with the Commander at Andrews Air Force Base. Because parts for it were scarce and some airports refused clearance because of its noise and exhaust, it had been retired after more than three decades in service. The aircraft symbolized his destiny. It was the first Air Force One. It had served eight presidents. The first was John F. Kennedy. He had commissioned its blue and white design; adopted the call sign "Air Force One"; and his body was flown home in it from Dallas after his assassination. Spaulding aspired to be a part of its legacy.

"I bet if you stood near a window on the right side," said Sugar, "I could see you."

"Sugar, I don't—" Spaulding jerked forward in his seat. "I think—"

"This is Captain Hastings again, we just hit a pocket of turbulence. I'll be taking the plane down some to avoid any more problems." His voice was even. "But just in case I can't fool mother nature, please take your seats and buckle up. If you haven't done so already."

"Are you coming over to the window?" asked Sugar. "I've got my 35mm camera. Maybe I can get a shot of you for the baby."

Spaulding glanced out of the windows. Rain drops ran down the small panes. His gut told him that something was off. He buckled his seat belt. "Look, the pilot just said . . ."

"Oh, come on," she said. "Get off your butt and come to the window."

"All right . . . all right." Unbuckling his seat belt, Spaulding rose, loosened his gray tie and walked to a window. He left his charcoal jacket draped over the back of the chair. He looked out of the window at a plane in the distance. He squinted, trying to make out her face. He couldn't see a damn thing, but he might as well humor her. "Wave, honey, so I can tell if it's you."

"Okay," she said. "I think I see you."

He heard the camera snap over the phone line and thought he saw a flash in a small window in her plane.

"Gotcha," she said.

"I—" Vice President Spaulding heard a loud explosion. He was knocked off his feet. The wind was kicked out of his lungs. He dropped the phone. He heard shrieks and chairs sliding around the room. He was hit in the face by papers and cards flying off the table. China crashed to the floor. Emergency alarms blared. He heard Sugar screaming his name. He saw the phone on the floor. It rolled out of his reach as the plane dropped altitude.

Spaulding struggled to his feet. He jammed his knee into the sharp edge of the table leg. "Damn!" A sharp pain shot through his leg. He grabbed the drawers of the wall cabinet and dragged himself to his feet, fighting against the steep angle of the plane.

His hazel eyes swept over Jack at the front of the plane. Jack bent over the Secretary of State and helped her to her feet. Senator Harlin was crumpled in a ball with his butt in the air. He glimpsed secret service agents rushing forward. Throughout the aircraft, senior officials were wide-eyed and disoriented as they staggered to a standing position.

Spaulding glanced out of the plane window into the darkness. Bright lights twinkled through the rain. He spotted the VH69 Blackhawk helicopters awaiting his arrival. His dark eyebrows gathered. "Je-sus!" They were too close to the airport. He could see the edge lights on parallel runways. His gaze dropped to the dark rough waters below. As the nose of the plane dipped, he was thrown into the wall cabinet. The cabinet's brass pulls dug into his skin. He felt blood trickled down his arm. The plane twirled in the sky. The wings rolled. He was tossed around the plane like a ragged doll. "I don't want to die," he whispered. All of the lights went out.

Air Force Two slammed into the tarmac and plowed through the large airport, crashing into everything in its path. The Vice President was thrown into a wall. His last thought was of his pregnant wife as a fiery ball of red and gold flames raced toward him.

Over the

Atlantic Ocean

MARK HASTINGS

Seconds before, Mark Hastings had clamped his sharp white teeth together as he shot horizontally through the dark rainy sky at one hundred miles per hour, the same speed as Air Force II right before it exploded. Within ten seconds, the pilot of Air Force Two was accelerating straight down, picking up an additional fifty miles per hour. Out of control, his legs whipped over his lean, muscular body as he free fell thirty thousand feet above the rough bluish-white waters of the ocean. He hadn't counted on the frigid sheets of rain. The icy water pelted his face and hands. He knew he was being blown off course, but he was powerless to do anything about it. He had barely gotten out of the jet in time. If he had delayed just three more seconds, he would be dead.

As Mark twirled out of control, he prayed. He prayed for forgiveness and he prayed for his life. His heart pounded against his chest as he fought to kick his legs into place. He had to get control of this thing. It was getting harder for him to breathe as the moisture in the air condensed on his exposed skin. He could barely breathe at this altitude. He needed more oxygen. He felt the burns on his face and neck from the blast as he tried desperately to reach the oxygen tank in his equipment bag. It wasn't there. He refused to panic. He figured he could free fall for about 80 seconds without it. After that, he would suffocate in the middle of all this air. It wasn't right. No one had forecasted rain. No one. Damn. From this height, it could be fatal. He flapped his cheeks against the brick-like air. Years of training had taught him to expand the surface area of his cheeks to absorb more O$_2$ through his skin. Because of his high speed, his body was being exposed to oxygen molecules at a higher rate than if he was walking on the ground below, which is where he wished to hell he was right now.

As he took in more air, his head cleared a bit. He focused on his grave predicament. The thirty-five pounds of equipment strapped to his back was whipping him around. If he didn't kick his legs back, he would eventually smack into the ocean surface like a gnat into a windshield. He would have smiled at the thought, except he wasn't ready to die.

As he whirled, he thought he glimpsed a white dot in the distance. No, not likely, he thought. The cavalry was not coming. He was on his own. As he spun again, he snapped his muscular quadriceps against his chest, executed a back loop, steadied himself and assumed a face-to-earth position. It slowed his rate of fall by 10-20 miles per hour. His hair, wavy and jet black, blew back from his tanned face. He relaxed a bit and his eyes, as dark as his hair, stared straight down as he assessed his situation. Below, the fiery crash lit up JFK airport. Apparently, Air Force II had split into three pieces. The fuselage had slammed into the airport, splitting in two. The tail section blazed as it sank into the Atlantic Ocean.

After he caught his breath and his heart rate slowed, he pressed his arms tightly against his side and thrust his head downward. In a deep dive, he shot toward earth at 350 miles per hour. Adrenalin rushed through his veins. As his ears popped, he aimed for the deep water in the bay near the airport. He planned to descend near a thicket of woods. He had left a fake passport, clothes and money there. He had also left evidence on the plane for the investigators. This was the last phase; the culmination of years of planning. He had spent ten years as a Navy pilot training, he now knew, for this moment. As a jumpmaster, he had done this hundreds of times before, although never from an exploding plane, never from this height and certainly never from the Vice President's plane. He had barely gotten out of the aircraft. The blast had been too soon. A mistake that had nearly cost him his life.

As Mark looked at the blaze below, he regretted the loss of life, except for one. Richard Spaulding. The Vice President thought that he was a better man; that he could take whatever he wanted and do with it what he pleased. Spaulding probably realized, too late, that he had lost. And Mark was certain that Spaulding had known why. Spaulding was shrewd. Mark would give him that much. Getting himself nominated and elected Vice President was no small feat. Spaulding had worked all of his familial and Senatorial connections to win the running mate slot and then had campaigned non-stop for months for the ticket. Later, he and his wife had labored to survive the scandal that was Roger Alexander. It had been considerably easier to get himself killed.

The icy cold rain penetrated Mark's blue pilot uniform. His skin felt cold and clammy even with the tech suit underneath the single zipper uniform. He checked his altitude gauges. He was at two thousand feet. A less skilled jumper would have deployed his parachute at least three thousand feet higher. Not him, he wanted to get as close to the ground as possible to avoid detection, but he wasn't interested in crashing either. He activated the opening sequence for his main parachute, yanked the ripcord and was snatched upward as the parachute deployed. As it opened up against the dark sky, he heard the ice flick off the square canopy parachute he always used. A stronger, lighter material, it was like an airplane wing with great aerodynamics; more like a glider than an umbrella. Mark was an expert jumper now and accustomed to the opening shock, but the sudden deceleration had scared the hell out of him during his virgin jump at a southern Naval Air base. In fact, he had nearly fainted. Who knew he had a weak heart? It had eventually forced him out of the service. As he glided downward, he squeezed the parachute's steering toggles, maneuvering closer to the shore.

Reaching into his equipment pack, he pulled out a scuba mask and slid it on. He wished he had his fins. The stiff black ones he had left on the plane gave his kick a lot more power.

But, at least, he was already wearing his weight belt and protection suit. His regulator, digital depth gauge and underwater compass were easily accessible in his back pack. He waited. The timing had to be perfect.

In the Navy, he had focused on two things. The intricacy of physics that skydiving and scuba diving required at this level; and the extreme risk of the two sports. He thought about both aspects as he glanced down at the dark waters below. The wind was picking up and the waters were getting rougher.

Just before his feet touched the cold water, he yanked hard on both of the parachute's steering toggles. He skimmed mere inches above the ocean surface for fifty yards and then braced himself for the dip of a perfect landing, but instead he got caught in a sudden gust of wind. Rather than releasing the parachute, he felt its limp nylon cords wrap around his arms and torso. Entangled, he slammed face first into the rough waters. The blast of cold water forced the air out of his lungs. He felt his collar bone snap. Disoriented, he plunged deeper. The heavy weight of the equipment dragged him further down into the icy depths. His body was instantly numb. Pain seared through his neck and shoulder as he tried to grab the cords. He struggled with the rope. His face mask was flooded. His cuts and bruises stung in the salt water. What the hell had happened to his oxygen tank? He had checked it twice. Had someone on the plane taken it? He had made sure everyone knew he would be diving in Kenya to divert any questions about the equipment. Again, he needed the tank. He was now suffocating for the second time in as many minutes.

As Mark sank deeper, he couldn't see anything. His eyes may as well as have been closed. His night goggles were in his back pack. The wet cords wrapped tighter around his arms and chest. Disoriented and in pain, he flung his arms and legs wildly. He wanted to scream in agony. As his lungs began to burn, he forced himself to calm down. He patted his chest. His numb index finger scrapped the single zipper of the uniform. He unzipped the pilot uniform and slipped out of it. It's seal, a gold and red Presidential emblem, floated by his mask. In a lined wet suit, he felt pounds lighter without the heavy equipment. Relief flowed through his body. He gave two strong scissors-kicks, away from the cords and parachute.

Fighting his way to the surface, Mark stroked hard with one arm, the other was limp by his side. He worried about sharks. He was vulnerable without his equipment. He stroked and stroked, but he couldn't break free of the water. Soon he would suffer cerebral and renal damage. He had to get out. His heart was beating out of control. If he didn't drown, he might be done in by cardiac arrest. He hadn't realized how deep he had sunk. His navigation equipment, high-tech and brand-new, was sinking to the ocean floor.

As his muscles grew fatigued and the pain grew worse, he thought briefly about giving up. He could simply surrender to the ocean. Maybe it wouldn't be that bad. He listened. The gentle reverberations of the ocean calmed him. The cold dulled his senses. As he let his weary arms drop to his side, his mind was effused with thoughts of her. He felt the touch of her creamy skin. He raised his arm and kicked again. He burst through the surface, gasping for air. Water streamed down his face. His dark hair was slick down against his forehead. Coughing and choking, he filled his burning lungs with cold air.

He was alive, he thought. *Thank God.* Exhausted and freezing, he treaded water for awhile, gathering his strength. His lips were bluish-white. The tips of his fingers felt pin-pricked. He flipped over onto his back and drifted. Shivering, he tried to ignore the pain. He looked up at the moon, full and luminous. He was grateful to be alive. He had lived for her. As he envisioned her face, a small smile crossed his lips. He possessed the damaged soul of the perfect woman. He didn't love her in spite of herself, but rather he was obsessed by the depth of her flaws. He was content only in her presence. He let the tide wash him up on shore. On the rocky coast, he lay motionless. He had made it. He was alive. Relief washed over him as the blue waters lapped up to his chest. His dark eyes drifted shut as sand shift beneath his back.

After some time passed, he heard sirens in the distance; probably ambulances and fire engines on their way. He realized he had lost track of time. He needed to hurry, but he was spent and he was hurt. He would rest for another minute and then grab his things out of the woods, get dressed and catch an international flight. His thick hair curled against his forehead. Without opening his eyes, he brushed it back. Catching his flight would be a bit more difficult now that JKF, the city's international airport, was damaged. Air Force II should have gone down in the Atlantic Ocean, but something had happened. Still, there were other ways to get out of the country. Then he would wait.

"Hello Mark."

Cool metal pressed against his forehead. His black eyes flew open. Had he been betrayed? He looked past the pearl handle of the small pistol into the eyes of his killer. His dark eyebrows gathered, perplexed. Maybe he wouldn't die tonight. As he blinked, a thousand questions flew through his mind. He settled on one.

"How did you know?" asked Mark.

"You're a creature of habit. And when I see you change your pattern, I ask myself 'why?'"

Mark smiled a charming, lop-sided grin and lifted his head from the sand. The pistol pressed him back down. He winced in pain as his collar bone twisted. He took a deep breath and asked, "Should I pray?"

"Prayer is for people who can't get the job done themselves." A thoughtful pause. "Would you rather die here or in the woods with your things?"

As Mark's grin faded, his weak heart beat faster. He stared at the short barrel. In his last seconds, he reflected on the flaws of his lover and on the power of retribution. "Here is fine." In the end, he didn't know if he died from a heart attack or the single gun blast.

THE LIST

Mr. Roger Alexander   Mr. Charles Thomas

Mr. Richard Spaulding   Mr. Mark Hastings

Look for
Act of Vengeance
Available Now!

www.Amazon.com
www.MillicentHodge.com
Wherever Hardcover Books are Sold

A Thriller Series

ABUSE OF POWER

by

Millicent Y. Hodge, Esq.

PROLOGUE

SPRING

STATEN ISLAND

F eeling overwrought, he peered up and down the narrow dirt road. He hesitated and then stepped into the thick underbrush. Twigs snapped beneath his black shoes. He moved forward tentatively, feeling his way in the cool haze of early morning. Armed with a heavy steel shovel, he brushed aside wild bushes and overhanging tree limbs as he walked right, hesitated, and then turned left. Was this the right way? In the distance, he heard something, maybe voices. He quickened his pace. Tree branches caught his cashmere sweater and clawed the forearm protecting his face. Blood trickled down the side of his neck. How had things gone so wrong?

Up ahead, he spotted a small creek. A red robin chirped, danced along the bank and stuck its beak into the tranquil stream. Yes, he was close now. Before, during the winter, the brook had been frozen solid. He crossed over it, sank ankle-deep in mud, cursed, but kept moving. Within minutes, a soft breeze carried the smell of death to him. He tracked the foul stench. His eyes scanned the underbrush and then paused. Partially wrapped in a patched quilt, it was lying on a bed of leaves and twigs, exposed now that the snow and ice had melted away. Insects buzzed at it. He stepped away, covered his face with his hands and felt the bile rise in his throat. The body had begun to thaw.

After his stomach settled, he grabbed the shovel and began to dig. The sound of dirt hitting dirt echoed in the woods. After a time, his body began to perspire. As he dug, his mind wandered to last winter. Late one night, the street lamps, just lit, had cast his long shadow along Centre Street as he rushed through whirling white drifts. Car tires had squealed, spinning on the icy downtown streets of Manhattan. He had checked his watch for the fifth time as he swept by a white courthouse, a dimly lit subway, and slender trees laid bare by the harsh winter. Ambushed by his own thoughts, he had stared past the few people sloshing by him. A soft flake had settled on his cheek, burning into his flesh. Shivering, he had pushed his cold hands deep in the pockets of his long black leather coat, crossed the empty park, and quickly climbed the white limestone steps to City Hall.

Inside, he had glanced around. Ahead of him, visitors placed their purses and keys on a conveyor belt. "Is the Mayor in?" he had asked the security guard posted at the entrance.

The guard had glanced up and nodded. "No, sir." He looked back down at the gray x-ray screen of the metal detector. "He left about fifteen minutes ago."

"Thanks, Fred." By-passing the metal detector, he stamped snow off his wet shoes onto a small mat before stepping onto the black-and-white diamond-patterned floor. He turned right, away from the Mayor's office. The muscles in his neck were tense as he rapidly scanned the faces in the large lobby of the elegant two-story, Federal-style building. Tourists and spectators, awaiting the public hearing upstairs, were milling about, admiring life-sized bronze statues and oil portraits.

As he crossed the lobby, he lifted his gaze up the twin spiral staircases toward the circular marble gallery, past the surrounding Corinthian columns, and up to the central dome, as was his habit. For a second, his gaze gently caressed the swags and rosettes meticulously carved into the dome. He closed his eyes and felt the hammering in his chest. He opened his eyes and glanced over his shoulder toward the west wing of the building. Where was the Mayor? He nodded to the receptionist, heard a click, and then pushed open a three-foot-high security gate. She had automatically activated the security release, opening the gate for him. As he passed her, he didn't notice her eyes trailing the length of his lithe body.

He strode down the east corridor and down several flights of stairs, black wing-tip shoes clicking against polished floors. On the landing, he slowed his pace to gather his composure. A thin line of sweat formed on his upper lip. What should he do with the body? Heart pounding, he entered the dimly lit room in the lower bowels of City Hall. Everyone was there. All eyes focused on him. "It's done."

As he finished digging, his thoughts returned to the present. He jammed the shovel upright into the ground and surveyed his work. A gunshot whistled past him through the trees. He hit the ground hard. Lying still, he listened. Silence. The chirping and buzzing had stopped. He slid over the muddy ground, closer to the shallow grave, and strained to see through the dense trees and bushes. Oh, god! Don't let me die. Not here. Not like this. His eyes darted in every direction, searching frantically. Sunrays filtered through the trees, glinting off the leaves. Finally, he spotted three men dressed in hunting gear with orange vests. They moved in his direction, carrying rifles. Were they following the rancid smell of dead flesh? With his heart pulsing in his ears, he crawled upward into a crouching position. The hunters stopped, argued and walked away. Breathing hard, he fled to his car, threw the muddy shovel on the Corinthian leather and slammed on the gas pedal.

Look for
Abuse of Power
Available Now!

www.Amazon.com
www.MillicentHodge.com
Wherever Hardcover Books are Sold

Author's Notes

Tobacco kills more Americans every year than AIDS, alcohol, car accidents, murders, suicides, drugs and fires combined.

Over 100 Americans sent to death row have been exonerated since 1973.

CBSNews.com | Lungcancer.org

ABCNews.com | Tobaccofreekids.org

About the Author

M illicent Y. Hodge is a graduate of Harvard Law School and Howard University, and has held senior positions in the political campaigns and administrations of a United States President and a New York City Mayor. She has served on various White House Task Forces in Washington, D.C., and delivered speeches at the White House, New York City Hall, the New York Federal Reserve, the U.S. Securities and Exchange Commission, and various universities. She has worked in large law firms in Manhattan and Atlanta. She has been admitted to practice law in New York, Washington, D.C., and Georgia. Ms. Hodge was raised in Arkansas. She is the author of suspense thrillers *Abuse of Power, Absence of Justice, Art of Retribution*, and *Act of Vengeance*.

Visit her website at www.MillicentHodge.com.

New Thriller Series	
	### Abuse of Power *They had a lot in common. He had a secret. She had a scandal.* In the spring, a dead body begins to thaw in the woods of Staten Island. The victim is linked to an explosive fire that kills sixty people. Taylor Mitchell is embroiled in scandal, along with her race for mayor of New York City and her engagement to a handsome businessman. In the resulting turmoil, he is not the only one exposed. In New York City, everyone has a secret. Softcover: 1-4134-1156-8 Hardcover: 1-4134-11576
	### Absence of Justice *She ran. They followed. Then he showed up.* The Attorney General is murdered in the Department of Justice. Helpless to save him, Sidney Cox, a young lawyer, races out of the building clutching a blood-stained FBI file. When she's arrested for the murder, a gifted attorney comes to her defense. Facing life imprisonment, she discovers death is only one misstep away. Softcover: 1-4010-7935-0 Hardcover: 1-4010-7936-9
	### Art of Retribution *It ended when he was captured. It began when he vanished.* A Presidential Aide is suspected of a murder he may not have committed. On his way to death row, he vanishes. Was he kidnapped or did he escape? During a massive manhunt, three others are kidnapped, including the U.S. Attorney prosecuting his case. What does Sidney Cox, a young lawyer, know? The kidnapper has perfected the art of retribution. Softcover: 1-4134-1158-4 Hardcover: 1-4134-1159-2
	### Act of Vengeance *The choice was passion or power. She picked one. He picked the other.* Cruising through a dark thunderstorm, Air Force Two explodes. Splitting into three pieces at six hundred miles per hour, the jet slams into Kennedy Airport, crashing into everything in its path. As a fireball of flames races toward the Vice President, his last thought is of his pregnant wife, Sugar. They both have secrets to hide and the murderer has committed the ultimate act of vengeance. Softcover: 1-4134-3171-2 Hardcover: 1-4134-3172-0

www.MillicentHodge.com | www.Amazon.com

Printed in the United States
16681LVS00001B/35